THE SPIDER:
THE DEVIL'S PAWNBROKER

THE DEVIL'S PAWNBROKER

By Grant Stockbridge

STEEGER BOOKS • 2020

PUBLISHING HISTORY

"The Devil's Pawnbroker" originally appeared in the May 1937 (Vol. 11, No. 4) issue of
The Spider magazine. Copyright 2020 by Argosy Communications, Inc. All rights
reserved.

CHAPTER 1
KNIVES BEHIND THE DOOR

THE PLAY was taut, exciting, full of suspense. Richard Wentworth, *alias* the Spider, sat in row B, with his fiancée, Nita van Sloan. They had coveted seats on the center aisle.

Wentworth glanced sideways at her, studied her beautiful profile. The short straight nose, the firm young chin, the delicate contour of her throat always intrigued him, and he never ceased to admire that profile. He felt her warm hand upon his, saw that she was keyed up, her eyes sparkling with emotional reaction from this powerful play that their friend Selden Rodman had written.

Neither of them knew that within a very few minutes they would both be plunged into a vortex of murderous drama that would cause this tense play to pale by comparison.

Both of these people were used to danger and to the menace of swift death. But at the moment they were absorbed in the make-believe world on the stage.

The play was definitely a success. Wentworth turned away from Nita, glanced at the distinguished first-night audience in the orchestra. The second act had just begun, and the influential critics were watching the stage, as spellbound as any callow schoolboy. They were being carried away by its strength, by the power of the theme, by the scope of the action.

The curtain went down for an instant to denote the passage

of time, and Nita van Sloan turned misty eyes to Wentworth. "It's wonderful, Dick, isn't it? I'm so glad for Selden. He deserves this success; he's worked so hard for it. 'Drums of Desire' is the greatest play of the year. It'll have a record run and the movies will buy it. Selden should make a half million out of it!"

Wentworth nodded. "Easily that, Nita. And he can use it. The

Wentworth twisted the Buriat's
knife hand, snatched the pistol,
and covered Mephisto.

last five or six years have been pretty bad for him. Alma deserves a break, too. She stuck with him through all their poverty, and raised their two children on almost nothing a week."

"Alma must be a very happy wife tonight," Nita said pensively. "I've often wondered how Selden managed to get money to support his family. He never borrowed."

Wentworth shrugged. "All that will be over now. His royalties will come in steadily. What I can't understand is that Selden

3

Rodman isn't here for the opening of the play." He nodded toward the box at the left. "There's Alma and the two kids, but Rodman hasn't shown up. They said he phoned that he'd been called out of town—"

He paused as an usher tapped him on the shoulder. "Mr. Wentworth, sir? You're wanted on the telephone. The man said you'd know who it was—that you left your seat numbers with him."

"Right." Wentworth gave the usher a quarter. "I'll be right there."

He started to get up, excusing himself to his beautiful companion. But Nita put a hand on his arm. Suddenly, there was a flicker of fear in her tawny eyes.

"Dick!" she said tautly, almost under her breath. "There's only one man who'd call you here—Ben Laskar!"

Wentworth avoided her eyes. "What of it, Nita—?"

"What of it!" she echoed. "It means that there's trouble somewhere. Ben Laskar is the contact man for the Spider. When people are in trouble, and want the Spider's help, they know they can get in touch with him through Ben Laskar." She dropped her voice to an even lower pitch. "And when Laskar calls you like this, it means that the Spider is going to walk again; that Richard Wentworth, wealthy sportsman and dilettante, will put on the cloak of the Spider, and risk his life again. And you promised me you were through, Dick!"

He lowered his glance before the reproach in her voice. It was true that whenever the Spider walked, Richard Wentworth risked his life. For the Spider fought crime, and the criminal underworld was aching to "get" the Spider. So were the police, for that matter. The mysterious cloaked figure whose twin blazing automatics had brought unconventional but deserved justice to so many czars of crime, was always in double jeopardy. His methods of fighting criminals were outside the law, and the law would not stand for it. So if the Spider were ever caught, he would surely take that slow walk to the electric chair.

Wentworth patted Nita's hand. "You're making a mountain out of a molehill, Nita. It may not be Laskar at all. And even if it is, it doesn't necessarily mean that the Spider will walk again. I'll answer the phone, and be back in a jiffy!"

Nita van Sloan was trembling as he got up and left her. Her eyes followed him up the aisle. Many women watched his handsome, athletic figure, with admiration. His sharply etched, hawk-like features, his broad shoulders and lean hips, brought many a flutter to the hearts of the women in the audience.

ON THE way up the aisle, Wentworth paused for a moment at Row E. A round-faced, pink-cheeked man of perhaps fifty, who sat in the aisle seat, waved to him.

"Hi, Wentworth! Aren't you staying? I thought it was a good show so far."

Wentworth smiled. "Hello, Mr. Blakely. How's the insurance business?"

Blakely laughed, as Wentworth bowed to Mrs. Blakely, who sat in the next seat. "Ha, ha. All I have to do with the insurance business these days is to attend Board of Directors' Meetings. By the way, Wentworth, you're a pretty heavy stockholder in the Orient Life Insurance Company; you'll be interested to know that we're sustaining heavy losses these days on suicides. May have to pass the dividend this quarter."

Wentworth's eyes narrowed. "I'd like to talk to you about that, Mr. Blakely. Maybe I'll call at your office tomorrow."

"Do that. I understand you do a little snooping around on

the side for a hobby—sort of amateur detective. You might look into the thing for the company. Make it noon tomorrow. I'll buy you lunch."

Wentworth nodded. "That's a date."

Mrs. Blakely smiled up at him. "We've been envying you and Miss van Sloan your seats. How did you get Row B? The theatre was sold out for the first night."

"I'm a friend of Selden Rodman's, Mrs. Blakely," Wentworth told her. "He sent me passes."

Mrs. Blakely was a warm, matronly sort of woman, who made no effort to hide the fact that she was a grandmother. "I'm so glad, for your friend's sake, that the play is a success. Tom and I would like to meet Mr. Rodman. Can you arrange it?"

"I'm sure he'll be glad to meet you and Mr. Blakely. He's out of town tonight, but perhaps you two will come to dinner some evening. I'll try to have him there. He's a wonderful chap, and deserves every bit of this success. And now, will you excuse me?

I see the curtain's going up, and I've still got to answer a telephone call. I'm afraid I'll miss part of this scene."

Wentworth started up the aisle again, with no suspicion that he was going to miss the rest of the entire play this night.

The lights were dimmed as he reached the lobby. The usher was waiting for him. "The phone is in the office downstairs in the lounge. This way, sir."

Wentworth followed the usher down. The lounge was deserted, and opposite the stairway he saw the open door of the manager's office.

"It's right in there, sir. If you'll excuse me, I'll go back on duty upstairs."

"Certainly," Wentworth said absently. His mind was on the few words that Thomas Blakely had let drop about the excessive losses of the Orient Life Insurance Company. It was not the possible loss of dividends that bothered him, but a vague sort of uneasiness about the recent series of suicides. He shrugged, stepped into the manager's office. The phone was on the desk, and the receiver was off the hook. He stepped toward it, and was abruptly conscious of a flurry of motion behind him.

Richard Wentworth was a man who had lived an adventurous and dangerous life. He was happiest with the odor of peril in his nostrils, and he was so used to quick physical action that it was almost second nature to him. And it was through a happy combination of agile mentality and swift physical reaction that he had been able to survive in his frequent conflicts with the underworld.

That slight hint of motion at his back was sufficient to key

7

him to tautness. His ears, suddenly tensed, caught the whistling of indrawn breath at his back.

There had been somebody waiting behind that open door!

WITH THE agility of rippling, well-conditioned muscles, Wentworth twisted to one side, flung himself to the floor. Another man might have hesitated at such unconventional action, for fear of making a fool of himself if it should turn out that there had been no danger. Not Wentworth. He *knew,* by that sixth sense that had made him a terror to the underworld, that there *was* danger.

And it was that quick action that saved his life.

There was a grunt, and a heavy body slid past him. The swish of a knife blade sounded clearly, and then the grating of steel against the mahogany desk, as the man who had lunged at him from behind missed, and went forward by his own impetus, to land against the desk.

Wentworth, on the floor, rolled over, while at the same time his right hand slipped up to his shoulder holster, came away with the flat, compact little twenty-five caliber automatic that he carried when he wore evening clothes.

He caught a glimpse of his attacker—a tall, raw-boned, slant-eyed Oriental, whose leathery skin gleamed greasily under the electric light. The man was swiftly pushing away from the desk, still gripping a long, straight-bladed dagger. From behind the open door, a second Oriental appeared, also gripping a knife. This one was much shorter than his companion, and squat, bow-legged. But he moved with wiry speed that made him a dangerous antagonist in a fight.

Wentworth recognized these types. They were not Chinese; Mongols of some sort. He had seen such men in Outer Mongolia, and around Lake Baikal. They were probably Buriats, the sole living devotees of the ancient religion of *Shamanism,* which had been largely

supplanted by Buddhism and Christianity in Mongolia. These men were fighters and killers from childhood, and he could see the hateful killer's gleam in their slant eyes now as they rushed him simultaneously, knives flashing upward for a death stroke.

They were both silent, lips tightly compressed, intent on finishing him quickly and without noise.

Though Wentworth had drawn his gun, he dared not shoot. The acoustic properties of this theatre building had been highly developed and even the short sharp bark of a small twenty-five caliber automatic would have been magnified to the proportions of a blast of thunder. He had seen the effects of such a shot upon theatre audiences in the past. Panics were easily caused, and people would be trampled, perhaps killed.

Instead of firing therefore, he used his gun to parry the thrusts of the Mongols. The taller one reached him first, and slashed down in a lunge that would have disemboweled him had it reached its mark.

Wentworth struck sharply with the barrel of the automatic, hit the man's wrist. There was a nasty, cracking sound. The Mongol snarled with rage and pain, retreated and dropped the knife, grimacing in agony, and holding his wrist with his left hand.

The second man came in at Wentworth in a flying leap, the blade of his knife held stiffly in front of him. The fellow's lips were parted in a snarl, and his eyes were red-rimmed with killer's lust.

Wentworth was on his knees now, and he swayed to one side, allowing the blade to slither past his shoulder, bury itself in the desk. At the same time he brought the barrel of the automatic down in a merciless blow upon the back of the fellow's head. The man sagged to the floor with a single grunt, and lay still.

The taller Mongol, with the broken wrist, had dived into his pocket, and produced a second knife, which he held by the tip, between thumb and forefinger of his left hand. He was poising it in the air, setting himself to throw it. These men were deadly with the throwing knife, Wentworth knew. If the blade ever left the Mongol's hand, it would speed toward its target too fast to avoid. Not even a bullet is harder to avoid than a knife thrown by an expert.

There was only a split-second of time between his glimpsing the man, and his action. Wentworth threw his automatic straight at the Mongol's face. There was little force behind the throw, for Wentworth had not had time to draw back his arm. He had merely flipped the gun up. It sailed through the air toward the man with the knife, who instinctively ducked to one side to avoid it; and in that instant. Richard Wentworth launched himself from the floor in a tackle that caught the Mongol just below the knees, sent him sprawling back into the wall.

Wentworth gave him no time to recover, but tangled with him on the floor, reaching up and seizing his left wrist. The man's right arm was useless, weakened by the first blow that Wentworth had given him; but he put up a vicious struggle for a moment, then relaxed, as if realizing the uselessness of fighting a stronger opponent.

He grunted, opened his hand and let the knife fall to the floor.

Wentworth smiled grimly, recovered his automatic, then got to his feet, and motioned the other to arise. The Mongol rose slowly to his knees, and suddenly swooped out, snatched up the knife he had just dropped, and lunged upward with it, in a deadly hamstringing blow.

Wentworth jerked backward, but the blade caught his trousers leg, ripped upward, gouging the skin of his thigh. Now the Mongol pushed to his feet, teeth showing in a fierce, murderous grin. He thrust straight at Wentworth's face, and Wentworth raised his left arm, took the full force of the blade in his forearm. The knife slashed through coat sleeve, ripped skin and flesh beneath. And Wentworth brought his right over in a smashing arc that crashed right into the Mongol's face, smashing the cartilage of his nose as if it had been paper.

The Mongol screamed, yanked at his knife, and tried another thrust. Wentworth sidestepped, drove his fist, gripping the automatic, into the man's stomach. The other doubled up, and Wentworth met his advancing chin with a beautifully timed uppercut.

The cracking impact of that blow sounded like the distant report of a rifle. The Mongol's head snapped up and backward, and he was literally lifted into the air. The back of his head smashed against the wall, and then he crumpled in a heap to the floor—out for the count.

Wentworth stepped back, drew out a handkerchief and held it to the cut in his arm. He looked up, and frowned.

Nita van Sloan stood in the open doorway!

SHE WAS panting, breathlessly beautiful. But she wasted no words, indulged in no hysterics. She had seen enough action and adventure with Wentworth to know that hysterics had no part in a fight. She had a gun in her hand, which she put back in her handbag when she saw the fight was over.

Swiftly she stepped forward, took the handkerchief from him, and helped him off with his coat. She did not even throw a second glance at the two inert Mongols on the floor. She worked with the quick efficiency of a trained nurse. A first aid kit, such as is prescribed for all theatres, hung in a white red-cross box from a hook in the wall. From this kit she got the necessary antiseptic and gauze, and swabbed out the wound, bound it expertly.

"I—I had to come after you, Dick," she said, as she worked. "Something told me there was trouble. You know how that intuition of mine always works." She looked up and smiled bravely. "You did a good job on those two. What did they have against you?"

He shrugged. "I don't know, Nita darling. They were waiting for me with knives when I walked in. It was touch and go for a minute. They look like Mongols, but I don't know where they're from, who sent them, or why they wanted to practice with their knives on me."

He glanced toward the desk. "There's the phone, still unanswered. Maybe that'll give us the answer."

With his free hand he picked up the receiver, said: "Hello, hello."

There was no answer. Slowly he put it down, and his eyes met Nita's. They were both thinking the same thing, and she put it into words.

"That phone call was a decoy, Dick, to bring you down here. This attack was elaborately planned. But why? You're not working on any case that I don't know about, are you?"

He laughed grimly. "I wasn't, Nita, five minutes ago. But I've got a case now. I'm going to find out who put these boys up to the knife work!"

Nita gripped his arm. "No, no, Dick!" She pressed hard, so that he winced. Her fingers were unconsciously on his fresh wound. "Leave it, Dick, please. You're giving it all up, aren't you? You promised me that you would. We're to be married next week, and sail for the Orient. Forget about this attack. You can stay at home for the week, and Jackson and Ram Singh will guard you—"

She broke off, seeing the thing in his eyes. Slowly she bowed her head, biting her lip. "I'm sorry, Dick. I should never have suggested that. It's a coward's way. I—I suppose I couldn't love you the way I do if you were the kind of man to hide away from danger."

A little sob caught in her throat. "I—suppose—you've got— to face it!"

13

He took her in his arms, pressed his lips against hers lightly.

"Stout girl, Nita. I've got to close this case. I couldn't marry you, knowing I was leaving unfinished business like this behind. The Spider has enemies. And since the last matter, when we fought it out with the Man from Singapore,* there are a number of people who know that Richard Wentworth is the Spider. If they've tried to kill me once, they'll try again—" his lips set grimly—"and I'm damned if I'll expose you to a life of constant danger after we're married!"

She lifted her chin bravely. "All right, Dick. You and I will fight this out together. What do we do now?"

He shook his head. "Not together, Nita. I won't want you taking any more chances. Let me take care of this—"

He stopped at sight of the stubborn set of her chin. "You'll not keep me out of it, Richard Wentworth!" she said firmly. I'm in this with you!"

He hesitated, threw her a queer glance. Then suddenly: "All right, Nita. Let's get out of here, before the manager comes down and discovers these boys. I don't want to have to give any explanations—especially when I don't know what to explain!"

---

* Author's Note: Wentworth here refers to the incident known as "The Scourge of the Yellow Fangs," which was related in the previous adventure. It was in solving the problem presented by the mark of the Yellow Fangs that Wentworth came to grips with the sinister Man from Singapore, and was forced virtually to admit his identity. Since then, he had been constantly expecting some such attack, once the word spread through the underworld that Richard Wentworth was the Spider.

HE TOOK her arm, was about to lead her out, when the phone on the desk began to tinkle. He snatched the receiver off before it should be heard outside, and said softly into the transmitter: "Yes?"

He at once recognized the voice at the other end. "May I talk to Mr. Richard Wentworth, please? He is in seat one or three, Row B. It's important—"

Wentworth cut the other short. "This is Wentworth, Laskar. What do you want?"

Ben Laskar was the Spider's contact man—the one whom men and women in trouble went to see when they wished to appeal for the Spider's aid. Until recently, Laskar had not known who the Spider was. But after the adventure of the Man from Singapore, Wentworth had deemed it wise to inform him. He trusted Laskar just as much as he trusted Nita, or his Sikh body servant, Ram Singh, or his World War hero chauffeur, Jackson.

At one time, Ben Laskar had been known as "Broadway's Honest Bookmaker." Honest Ben had handled wagers running into the hundreds of thousands, and he had always paid off. Ben Laskar's word had been as good with all Broadway as the word of the strongest bank in the country—no, even stronger; for no one ever needed a receipt for money left with him, and he always settled disputes by giving the other fellow the benefit of the doubt.

But misfortune had struck. Laskar had been framed for a crime he did not commit, and sent to prison. Released, he had become involved in the toils of a super-criminal whom the Spider was battling. Wentworth had gotten Laskar out of the

15

difficulty he was in, had set him up in an office of his own, ostensibly back in the bookmaking business, but really as the contact man for the Spider. And now, Laskar was calling, with a frantic note of panic in his voice.

"Mr. Wentworth!" the little bookie said over the phone. "For God's sake, watch out. Someone is planning to kill you!"

Wentworth laughed. "I know that, Ben. But the plan went haywire. What do you know about it? Talk quick; I've just put two gentlemen to sleep, and I want to go away from here."

"They came into the office here, Mr. Wentworth—three of them. I had just put the telegram from Mrs. Sabin in the safe—"

"What telegram?" Wentworth rapped.

"A telegram arrived this evening, from a Mrs. Norman Sabin, in Midwest City. She claims she's in trouble, and wants to contact the Spider. Shall I get it out and read it—?"

"No, no, never mind. I'll come over and read it myself. What happened after the telegram arrived?"

"I put it in the concealed wall safe, and got out the slip of paper which you left here, saying where you'd be tonight. I was just dialing the number, when these three men came in. One was a white man, and the other two were some kind of Chinese. Before I could move, they pulled guns on me, and they had me tied up in a jiffy. They gagged me, too, and I could hear them talking in some strange kind of language. They must have found the slip of paper, because I heard one of them repeat the phone number. They had hit me on the head, and they thought I was unconscious, so they didn't mind talking."

"I see," Wentworth said slowly. "Would you recognize that white man if you saw him again?"

"No, sir. He wore some sort of handkerchief—all black—over his face, and you could only see his eyes. But I heard him give directions to the two Chinese, as to how to get to the theatre. He was talking in that foreign language, but I recognized the name of the theatre, and he mentioned the play, 'Drums of Desire.' Then the two Chinese left, and the white man waited a while, then dialed a number. After he got it, he asked for you. Then he hung up, and left. He didn't even bother to look at me. I worked free, and called you up!"

"Hmm," Wentworth mused—"You're lucky, Ben. Hang on there—I'll be right over."

HE REPLACED the receiver, looked at Nita. "You were right, dear. It was a deliberate plant to get me down here. And there's a white man giving orders. Let's go. I'm afraid we won't be able to see Selden Rodman's play, after all!"

He led the way upstairs. In the lobby, they passed a large poster, which read:

DRUMS OF DESIRE
A Drama
in
Three Acts
by
Selden Rodman

He grimaced. "Isn't life queer, Nita! Selden has spent five years going through the hell of poverty; he writes a single play, and he's fixed for life—nothing to worry about. And here are we—we've been having a wonderful time in the past years; and now we've got to pay for it by being marks for greasy Mongols with knives. And yet—I wouldn't change places with Selden!"

"I know, Dick!" Nita touched his arm understandingly. "You wouldn't be happy if you didn't have things happening to you like the thing that just happened downstairs. I sometimes think—" her voice became wistful—"that I'd like to have a husband like Selden Rodman. There wouldn't be any of this danger, this constant fear that the man I love will be found in some alley with his throat cut—"

She stopped, staring wide-eyed across the lobby.

Jack Lawson, Selden Rodman's literary agent, was standing in the doorway. He had apparently been called from his seat to accept a telegram, had signed for it, and was reading it, while the Western Union messenger waited to see if there would be an answer. And suddenly, Lawson uttered a strangled cry, and staggered, reached for support to the wall. His face had gone as white as paper.

Wentworth leaped across the lobby, caught him by the arm. "What's the matter, Jack? Stand up, man!"

Lawson looked up, shuddered. "My God, it can't be true! Mr. Wentworth! Read that, for God's sake, and tell me if I'm seeing right!"

Wentworth took the telegram, glanced at its contents. His lips tightened, and his eyes became suddenly bleak. The telegram was dated that evening from Midwest City, and read:

JACK LAWSON
  C/O DRAMA THEATRE
  NEW YORK, N.Y.
  YOUR CLIENT SELDEN RODMAN COMMITTED
  SUICIDE HERE AT EIGHT P.M. CENTRAL TIME
  STOP HE SHOT HIMSELF IN LOBBY OF ALAMEDA
  HOTEL IN PRESENCE OF DOZEN WITNESSES STOP
  LEFT NOTE DIRECTING GET IN TOUCH WITH
  YOU STOP PLEASE WIRE INSTRUCTIONS WHAT
  TO DO WITH BODY OR SEND REPRESENTATIVE
                    CLARKSON,
                    CHIEF OF POLICE

Silently, Wentworth handed the form to Nita.

Lawson was groaning: "It's impossible. It couldn't have happened. My God, Rodman was just on the threshold of success. I wired him at the Alameda Hotel that his play was a hit. He must have got the wire just before he shot himself. He had everything to live for. He loved his wife and kids, and he was going to have loads of dough. Why should he do it?"

Wentworth was thinking fast. Ben Laskar, the bookmaker, had said that there was a telegram in the office from a Mrs. Norman Sabin, in Midwest City. Had it anything to do with the suicide of Selden Rodman? Had it anything to do with the attack by those two Mongols in the manager's office downstairs? Abruptly he felt himself being drawn irresistibly into a vortex of mystery which would take him—where?

His fingers tightened on Jack Lawson's arm. "Buck up,

Lawson. It must be the truth. You've got to face it. What are you going to do?"

Lawson was inclined to be a bit stoutish, with a soft, flabby face, and thinning, nondescript hair. His lower lip was trembling. "I—I don't know, Wentworth. I—don't know. I—I'm all broken up!"

"Well, pick up the pieces!" Wentworth rapped drily. "Are you going to Midwest City?"

"I—I guess I'll have to. I—someone will have to tell Alma Rodman. She's in there, so happy, sitting in the box with her two children, enjoying her husband's triumph. And now—"

"All right!" Wentworth cut him short. "Talking like that isn't going to help. Here—" he thrust the telegram at Nita—"you're the logical one to break the news to Alma. I know it's a tough assignment, dear, but you'll have to do it."

Nita forced a smile. "I'll try to tell her. And what are you going to do, Dick?"

"I'm going to Laskar's office. Then I'm going home. When you get through with Alma Rodman, take her home, then go to your apartment, and wait for a message from me. And while you're taking her home, you might try to find out from her why Selden Rodman went to Midwest City, today of all days!"

Nita nodded. "Right, Dick. And remember, I'm in on everything. You've got to count me in."

She took the telegram, and went into the dark theatre, where Alma Rodman would be watching the second act of her husband's successful play, all unconscious of the dreadful news she was about to hear.

20

Wentworth sent away the Western Union messenger, and swung to Jack Lawson. "Look here, Jack! I want you to go and pack your bags. There's an eleven o'clock train leaving for Midwest City. Meet me at Pennsylvania station, at the information booth, at ten minutes of eleven. I'm going with you!"

Lawson's mouth opened in surprise. "You—why, Wentworth? Why in God's earth do you want to—?"

"Because," Wentworth told him tightly, "in spite of the fact that Selden Rodman shot himself in a public place, in the presence of dozens of witnesses, the story doesn't ring true. I intend to find out why a man on the threshold of success and fame should have taken his own life!"

CHAPTER 2
MEPHISTO'S WARNING

B EN LASKAR'S office was on the eighth floor of the Variety Building, on Broadway just above Times Square. There was another entrance to this office, through another building on the side street, but Wentworth disdained to use it. If he were being followed, he wanted his shadow to know just where he was. If another attempt was to be made upon his life, he wanted it to be made quickly. The sooner he came to grips with his shadowy opponent, the better he would like it.

On the way out of the Drama Theatre, he had put Jack Lawson in a cab, then he had gone to the corner, found the patrolman on the beat, and told him that he had heard shouts from the Drama Theatre and that someone had told him there were robbers in the manager's office. The patrolman would find the two Mongols, and place them under arrest on suspicion, if for nothing else. They would be safe in jail overnight, where Wentworth could have them questioned—though he entertained little hope of extracting any information from those two.

On the way from the theatre, he had watched the cab's back trail, and had noted a car which had kept pace with them all the way to the Variety Building. It might be someone shadowing him, and then again it might be a coincidence. He didn't bother to check up. For the time being he assumed that he was being followed, and acted accordingly.

The Variety Building is occupied fifty percent by theatrical and sporting enterprises of one kind or another, and there are always people going in and out. Many of the offices are open into the wee small hours of the morning, so that it was not strange for him to be coming here at this hour.

He stopped off at the cigar counter, spoke to the night man in charge. "Look here, Joe, I think someone is following me. If you should notice any one here in the lobby who shows any interest in what floor I went to, be a good fellow, and phone up to me in Ben Laskar's office."

He slipped Joe a ten-dollar bill, and the man winked. "Trust me, Mr. Wentworth. I'll keep the old eagle eye peeled!"

Upstairs on the eighth floor, Wentworth entered the office marked:

BEN LASKAR
Investments

Laskar was short, wiry, with an old-young countenance. He was seated at his desk, toying with a length of rope.

"Hello, Mr. Wentworth," he greeted. "I was certainly a prize sap, letting those guys get the drop on me." He winked. "But they overlooked the cigar cutter in my vest pocket. I worked it out, and cut the ropes! Gosh, what a sap I was! Those Chinese might have killed you—and I'd never have forgiven myself—"

"They weren't Chinese, Laskar, they were Mongols. And don't be too hard on yourself. Anyone can make a mistake. Now forget it, and give me that telegram from Mrs. Norman Sabin."

He took the precaution to lock the corridor door while Laskar was getting the telegram out of the wall safe.

"At least it's a good thing I put it in here," Laskar chuckled. "They went through the desk and the filing cabinet, but they didn't think to look behind this medicine cabinet!"

The wall safe was a small one, cleverly concealed behind the medicine cabinet over the sink. The whole cabinet lifted off its hook on the wall, revealing the small knob of the safe. It was here that Laskar kept his operating funds—always a sizeable amount in cash.

Wentworth seized the telegram, unfolded it swiftly. As he read, his brow furrowed in perplexity. There was much more to this suicide business than he had at first suspected.

BEN LASKAR
    VARIETY BUILDING, NEW YORK
    MY FAMILY ATTORNEY HAS GIVEN ME YOUR
    NAME AS THE SPIDERS CONTACT MAN STOP I

AM AFRAID MY HUSBAND IS GOING TO COMMIT SUICIDE LIKE THE OTHERS THE PAPERS HAVE REPORTED IN LAST FEW WEEKS STOP IT IS TERRIBLE KNOWING IN MY HEART HE IS GOING TO KILL HIMSELF AND NOT BEING ABLE TO DO ANYTHING TO PREVENT IT STOP ONLY THE SPIDER CAN SAVE HIM STOP FOR GODS SAKE BEG THE SPIDER TO COME AND HELP ME STOP I WILL GIVE HIM ANYTHING HE ASKS IF HE WILL ONLY COME STOP WIRE ME COLLECT IF SPIDER AGREES TO COME STOP ADDRESS IS TWO TWENTY TWO NORTH ALAMEDA DRIVE MIDWEST CITY STOP IN THE NAME OF GOD HELP ME.

MRS. NORMAN SABIN.

WENTWORTH FROWNED over the message. "Two twenty-two North Alameda Drive—the Alameda Hotel must be on the same street. And Selden Rodman just committed suicide there. Now this."

Laskar whistled. "Rodman a suicide! He's a friend of yours, isn't he, Mr. Wentworth?"

"Yes. But I don't know this Sabin—"

Laskar grinned. "After I got free of the ropes, I figured

RICHARD WENTWORTH

you'd be wanting to know something about him, so I called a friend who works in the morgue of the New York *Daily Star*. He looked it up for me. Norman Sabin is a leading physician in Midwest City. A few years ago he wasn't so wealthy, but he struck it rich in the stock market or something, and now he's in the social register. He's the director of a bunch of corporations, and he's also the director of the medical staff of the Orient Life Insurance Company—"

"*What?*" Wentworth snapped his fingers. "Of course! Midwest City—that's the home office of the Orient Life! And I was just talking to Thomas Blakely tonight and he told me they've been sustaining heavy losses through suicides!"

Ben Laskar whistled. "Gosh, Mr. Wentworth, this sounds all tangled up. But why should they be putting the bee on you? You got nothing to do with it, except that you know Rodman—"

The phone rang, and Wentworth said: "That may be Joe, downstairs. Let me take it."

He picked up the instrument, said: "Yes?"

A silky voice replied: "Am I speaking to Mr. Wentworth?"

Wentworth felt a sudden chill of menace. This was not the voice of any ordinary man. From just those six words he was able to tell it. There was a wealth of power, of malice, of evil in that voice; and withal a degree of culture and of poise that made its owner doubly dangerous.

Wentworth waved to Laskar to get on the other phone and trace the call. Then he spoke into the transmitter: "Who is this?" he asked.

"For the time being," the voice replied, still retaining its quality of steel clothed in silk, "you may call me Professor Mephisto. Later, perhaps, we shall become better acquainted—though I sincerely trust, for your sake, that you will make such acquaintance unnecessary."

Wentworth watched Laskar calling the telephone company to trace the call. He tried to stall for time.

"Professor Mephisto!" he said musingly, as if thinking aloud. "That's a strange name nowadays. Are you the gentleman who directed the attack on me at the Drama Theatre tonight?"

"Ah, that. That was quite unfortunate. Had my two friends been more competent, I should not now be telephoning you."

"I'm very sorry," Wentworth said drily, "that I couldn't accommodate your friends by permitting them to insert a length of steel between my shoulder blades. Now is there anything else I can do for you—that is, anything reasonable?"

"I'll tell you, Mr. Wentworth," Mephisto said confidentially—"or, shall I call you—Spider?"

"You'd better call me Wentworth. I don't know anyone who was born with a name like Spider."

Mephisto chucked. "Very clever, Wentworth, but highly casuistic. But let's not beat about the bush any longer. As I expected you would, you are interfering in a certain undertaking of mine. I should greatly appreciate it if you would withdraw from the matter entirely. After all, you are not involved in any way—"

"Except that I don't like being rushed with knives."

"Quite so. I will admit that was an error. I should have approached you in this way first. But then, you might have realized the extent of my power. Now that you know, perhaps you will be willing to give me your word not to mix into this thing any further? I am prepared to accept the verbal promise of the Spider. You see, I know your reputation."

"And if I refuse to promise?"

"Then, Mr. Wentworth, I shall be regretfully compelled to take other steps. In fact, those steps have already been taken, in the event of your refusal. Permit me to outline them. First, another attempt will be made upon your life. It will be made in a much more thorough fashion than the first, you understand. That affair at the Drama Theatre was merely by way of warning."

"I see. But if I had taken that warning in the ribs—"

Wentworth was talking desperately, trying to keep the man on the wire, for he saw that Laskar was having trouble in tracing the call.

Mephisto interrupted him. "Ha, ha. That was a clever remark. I begin to think that I have underrated you. Had you taken that warning in the ribs, as you put it, everything would have been simplified. Now let me proceed, for I would like to finish before you succeed in tracing this call."

Wentworth started. The man was far from a fool.

"You see, Mr. Spider, I have prepared for every contingency. If my next attempt upon your life fails, I shall try another angle. Every man has his Achilles' Heel. In your case, it would be that beautiful young lady, Miss Nita van Sloan. If you should be able to protect yourself against my attempt, I would then concentrate upon her. I'm sure you would not like to see that beautiful young woman's body limp and lifeless, eh?"

Wentworth's knuckles whitened on the phone. He was willing to take his own chances; but to make Nita the brunt of an attack—

He mastered his sudden, overwhelming rage at his suave fiend, and said in a cool voice: "I suppose it wouldn't be any good to try to convince you that I am not the Spider?"

Mephisto laughed. "Everything points to Richard Wentworth as being the Spider. There is only one way that would convince me, and would cause me to forget Miss van Sloan."

"Yes?"

Mephisto's voice grew even more silky. "If Richard Wentworth were to be killed or incapacitated, and if then the Spider were to appear, I would be convinced that I had misjudged you. Otherwise, my friend, I will continue to believe that you are he. And now—the answer. Will you give me your promise?"

Laskar turned away from the other phone, raising his hands in despair. "They can't trace the call, boss," he whispered. "The line Superintendent thinks he must be tapping in on a wire somewhere!"

Wentworth hid his disappointment.

Mephisto was repeating his demand: "Your promise, please!"

Wentworth put his mouth close to the phone. His voice

was husky with emotion. "I'll promise you this, Professor Mephisto—that if Miss van Sloan is harmed in any way, *I'll track you down to the ends of the earth, and break your back with my bare hands!*"

There was an angry *cluck* at the other end, and the line went suddenly dead.

WENTWORTH HUNG up. His jaw was set firmly. "Another attack on me," he muttered, "then they go after Nita. And he meant every word of it, too!"

He raised his eyes to the little bookmaker. "It's war, Laskar. And the odds are on the other side!" His fists clenched. "Professor Mephisto, eh? I wonder what his game is!"

Laskar was leaning over the desk. "It's bad, boss. The guy knows you're the Spider, and he knows about Miss Nita; but you don't know a thing about him!"

"I intend to find out!" Wentworth said grimly. "First, I'm going to make sure nothing happens to Miss van Sloan." He dialed the number of his own penthouse duplex apartment on Central Park West, and in a moment he was talking to his Sikh servant, Ram Singh.

Ram Singh had been in his service through many an adventure, and recognized every mood of his master's. The Sikh was a top-notch fighting man in his own right, being descended from a long line of fierce warriors. Yet he deemed it no disgrace—in fact he was proud—to be serving a man like this master of his. Jackson, the chauffeur, had been a sergeant in the A.E.F., in Major Wentworth's outfit. Both these men knew how to obey orders, and they did not question Wentworth now as he gave swift instructions.

"Ram Singh! Miss van Sloan is in great danger. Take Jackson and go at once to her apartment. Do not leave her, either of you, on any condition. Guard her carefully. And look out for Mongols. I have no time to explain now. Miss van Sloan will tell you everything you need to know."

"*Wallahi,* master!" Ram Singh's voice was edged with eagerness. "Is it to be another fight? And did you say Mongols? I shall have a chance to whet my blade once more in throats of pigs!"

"I hope you don't get the chance, Ram Singh!"

"And what of you, master? Shall you need help?"

"No. I'll handle this myself. You'll hear from me."

He hung up, and already the germ of an idea was fertilizing in his mind; but he didn't know how to carry it out. For a long time now he had grappled with the question of how to keep Nita, and Ram Singh and Jackson, from being exposed to danger through their association with him. Those three would go through fire for the privilege of fighting at his side; and that was precisely what he didn't want. He must take some measures to keep them safely out of harm's way while he broke a lance with Professor Mephisto.

He looked up, to find Laskar anxiously waiting for orders. Immediately he dismissed all thoughts from his mind but the immediate plan of action.

"Ben! I'm going to Midwest City. You will handle things at this end. If Nita, or Ram Singh, or Jackson, should ask you where I am—"

Laskar smiled knowingly. "I can be a clam all right, boss. I haven't seen you for a week!"

Wentworth nodded. His left arm, where the Mongol's knife had gouged him, was a little stiff, but he paid it no attention. "Here's what I want you to do. In the first place, get out of this office; it's no good any more. Mephisto will keep too close tabs on it from now on. You go to the Coast Hotel, on Forty-eighth Street, and check in as Mr. Sanders."

"I get you, boss."

"You'll operate from there. Call a reliable detective agency. Have them put a tail on Thomas Blakely, president of the Orient Life Insurance Company; on Alma Rodman, Selden Rodman's widow; and on Jack Lawson, Rodman's agent. I want their every move reported. Understand?"

"Right, boss." Laskar jotted down the names.

"Also, I want inquiries made among the foreign colonies in the city, as to the presence of any unusual numbers of Mongols. That shouldn't be so hard to do, because there aren't many of them in New York. I'll want to know when they came, and who was instrumental in getting them admitted into the country. They must have had to put up a bond at Ellis Island; find out who gave the bond. Prepare your reports, and I'll wire you from Midwest City, or else call you on the long distance."

"Right, boss. Everything's clear. And I think we better leave through the other building."

Wentworth nodded. He was at the closet, busy changing from his tuxedo to a gray business suit, which was one of a half dozen hanging there. He strapped on a double shoulder holster under his jacket, and provided himself with a pair of grim-looking, heavy-caliber automatics from a locked strongbox compartment in the closet.

He also withdrew from the closet a small flat case which was cunningly fitted with a mirror, several tubes of pigment and plastic material, and nose and mouth plates as well as tufts of vari-colored hair which could be used for eyebrows and moustache. In short, that case contained all the material necessary for a complete disguise.

Another flat leather case contained a selection of chromium tools, which had been made especially to Wentworth's order. That kit had more than once gotten the Spider out of a tight spot.

Last of all, he brought out a small parcel containing a black cape and black slouch hat. These were the familiar habiliments of the Spider. That caped figure had long been a symbol of terror to the underworld, and to criminals in high places. Wentworth had thought, when he made his plans to marry Nita, that he would never wear that cape and hat again. But Professor Mephisto had appeared on the scene; and the Spider was destined to walk once more!

Through a secret passage behind the wall of the closet, Wentworth led the way out. This passage led them across a narrow, blind shaftway, perched perilously on a plank, into an office in the building around the corner. From here they descended swiftly to the street, and parted—Laskar to register as Mr. Sanders at the Coast Hotel, and Wentworth to hurry to his Central Park West penthouse apartment.

Neither of them could have foretold the burden of misery, torture, agony and death that the next twenty-four hours were destined to bring....

CHAPTER 3
AMBUSH ON THE LAWN

WENTWORTH'S PENTHOUSE apartment was located on the roof of an apartment building which he owned. To all outward aspects, it was no different from any of the other swank structures along Central Park West; and he himself had the reputation of being a wealthy young man who had invested a portion of his capital in real estate, in order the better to enjoy the pleasures of life.

He was known as a benevolent landlord, and nothing was too good for his tenants in the way of service. Among those tenants were several judges of the state, some of the most prominent attorneys in the city, an assistant District Attorney of New York County, and the Police Commissioner of the City of New York.

It was characteristic of the cleverness with which Wentworth had planned the construction of this building that none of these tenants suspected that the structure was in many respects a fortress. The walls were reinforced with concrete, and there were cunningly contrived openings at intervals in the walls, which looked like ornaments but were in reality loopholes through which rifles could be fired in the event of an attack. The doors opening into the street resembled opaque glass, but were really made of thin sheet steel.

The doorman, the elevator operators, and all the other employees of the building were in every case ex-service men who had fought in Wentworth's regiment in the World War. They were dependable, trustworthy, and ready to fight for their employer if necessary—though none  of them suspected that, on the occasions when he was away for several days at a time, he was wearing the cape and hat, and using the twin automatics of the Spider.

Wentworth's apartment was on the roof. It was of the duplex type, and the lawn which had been landscaped onto the roof in front of his doorway was a masterpiece of artistry. One of the elevators from the main floor served the roof, opening onto his lawn. From here one crossed the lawn, through a path lined with umbrella trees, toward the apartment. That elevator was for Richard Wentworth and his visitors.

For the Spider, however, there was another entrance known to none but Wentworth, Nita, and a few of the trusted employees. Access to this secret entrance was obtained through an alley alongside the church on the street directly behind the building. This alley led to a row of garages in the back yard, which were provided for the use of the tenants. Garages one, two, three and four were reserved for the owner. Here he always kept several cars, ready for instant use. Also, in the floor of each of these individual garages was a cleverly concealed trapdoor, leading into the basement of the building. Here a small, high-speed elevator carried one directly up to the interior of the penthouse apartment. In such fashion did the Spider come and go, when necessary.

Now, however, Wentworth used the main entrance. He frowned, upon alighting from his cab, to note that the doorman was not on duty. In the lobby, only one of the two elevators was in service, and his eyes narrowed at sight of the operator. This man was not one of his regular employees. The man appeared to be thoroughly trained, for he slid the door of the cage closed, asked in a carefully respectful voice: "What floor, sir?"

Wentworth studied the operator for a moment. He was a husky type, with broad shoulders, thick arms and neck, and a square jaw.

Wentworth asked him: "Where's the regular operator?"

The man half turned. "Oh, he had to go home, sir. His wife was sick. The agency sent me up to relieve him."

"What's your name?"

"John Franco, sir."

"What agency did you come from?"

The man hesitated, then swung around pugnaciously. "Say, what's it your business, anyway, mister? The super hired me. I don't have to give the history of my life to every tenant. You goin' to the penthouse?"

Wentworth asked him softly: "How did you know I wanted the penthouse?"

"I—ah—I guessed it. I just took a guess, is all."

"You're a pretty good guesser. Where's the doorman? Is his wife sick, too?"

The operator snarled. "You're asking too many damn questions—"

"You'll answer them!"

"Like hell I will. You're only a tenant—"

Wentworth smiled bleakly. Professor Mephisto had slipped up.

HE HAD no doubt now that this operator was in the employ of Mephisto, and that this was the threatened second attempt upon his life. But Mephisto had not discovered that Wentworth was the owner of the building. A search of the records would not have disclosed that fact, for the building was registered in the name of a corporation. They had not expected that the presence of a new elevator operator would arouse their intended victim's suspicions to this extent.

And the man, Franco, must have sensed that his imposture was discovered. For he suddenly bared his teeth in a snarl, and his hand leaped toward his shoulder holster.

But Wentworth stepped in close, brought up his right fist in a smashing blow to the man's jaw. Franco crashed back against the wall of the cage, emitted a deep sigh, and crumpled to the floor. The back of his head was bloody. His skull must have been fractured against the steel wall.

Wentworth glanced down at him thoughtfully. He was sure now that the doorman and the regular elevator had been forcibly removed from here. But where?

On a hunch, Wentworth ran the elevator down into the basement, reaching over the body of the unconscious Franco to manipulate the lever.

His hand leaped to his holster,   but Wentworth stepped in close.

He stepped out into the basement, and at once he found what he sought. Three figures squirmed on the floor, cruelly bound with picture wire. They were the night engineer, the doorman and the elevator operator.

Swiftly, Wentworth undid the wire, freed them. All three of them nursed wounds or bruises. Quickly, he got the story out of them.

A car had pulled up at the entrance, and the doorman could have sworn that the man who descended from it was Richard Wentworth. He was accompanied by three other men, who all entered the lobby with him. The doorman said he had wondered why Wentworth was not using one of his own cars, but had not thought it important.

Then the doorman had suddenly heard himself called by name from the elevator. He entered the cage with the operator and the four men, only to find himself staring into the muzzles of four revolvers.

It was then that he got a good glimpse of the man who was posing as Wentworth, and realized that the resemblance was due to clever makeup. In the darkness outside he had made the natural mistake of believing this man to be his employer.

Both he and the elevator operator realized that this must be more than a holdup—that it must be a plot against Wentworth. They attempted to put up a struggle, but they were outnumbered, and quickly subdued by blows from the weapons of the intruders. Then they were brought down to the basement, where the night engineer was likewise overcome. The three of them were bound with the picture wire, gagged, and left here. That was all they knew.

Wentworth pursed his lips. "Those four chaps," he mused, "must be up on the lawn, or else in the apartment."

"They couldn't get in the apartment, sir," the doorman told him. "Ram Singh and Jackson left about a half hour ago, and Ram Singh always locks up carefully when he leaves the apartment alone. I doubt if anyone could get past those locks you've installed."

Besides Ram Singh and Jackson, there was the butler, Jenkyns, an old servant who had worked for Wentworth's father. But Jenkyns' health had been bad of late, and Wentworth had sent him away to the country. This left the penthouse apartment entirely unguarded, except by the elaborate system of locks and photoelectric rays which Wentworth had installed. He was sure that the marauders could not have entered the apartment. Therefore, they must be somewhere in the building, or else on the lawn on the roof. If they were on the lawn, he had a pretty good idea of their purpose.

"All right," he said. "I'm going up through the back entrance. Get this fellow out of the elevator, tie him up and take him into the employees' First Aid room. Get back to your posts, and act as if nothing had happened. Don't call the police, don't mention this incident to anyone. Phone to Doctor Maxwell, and have him come here to patch this chap up. I don't want him taken to a hospital. The First Aid room has all the equipment necessary. Keep him here till he's conscious, and then see what information you can get out of him. Anything you learn, phone it to a

Mr. Sanders, at the Coast Hotel. That's all."

HE LEFT them to carry the unconscious thug out of the cage, and made his way to the rear of the basement, stepped through a storage bin, and pressed a spot in the wall. A panel slid back to reveal a small self-service elevator. In a moment he was whisked up to the penthouse apartment.

He came out into the rear hall of the ground floor of the duplex, and made his way carefully toward the front. Peering out of one of the barred windows, he nodded in satisfaction. His judgment had been correct.

Four shadowy figures were moving about on the lawn, close to the main elevator shaft. In the light from the low-watt bulbs around the roof, he could see the glint of guns in their hands. Though these men were clearly visible from the penthouse apartment, they were screened by the shrubbery from anyone who might emerge from the elevator.

Wentworth smiled grimly. He understood just how clever Professor Mephisto was. The man had deliberately phoned him, threatening Nita. Mephisto must have expected that he would order his personal servants to go and guard Nita, leaving the apartment unwatched. He had banked upon that in his death scheme to attack Wentworth on his own roof.

He stood now for several minutes, watching those four men. They were apparently settled here for a long vigil. With their man running the elevator, they could afford to wait all night, if necessary, for Wentworth's return.

Wentworth wondered just why the unknown Professor Mephisto was so anxious to eliminate the Spider. There was no doubt now in his mind that Mephisto was in some fashion connected with the inexplicable suicide of Selden Rodman in Midwest City. Had Mephisto's interest in the Spider been brought about by the knowledge that Wentworth was Rodman's friend, and would pry into the playwright's death? Or was it because Mrs. Norman Sabin had appealed to the Spider for help?

Whoever Mephisto was, he must be wealthy, educated, clever. He must command large resources to be able to enlist the services of thugs like these, and of the queer, knife-wielding Mongols. Wentworth determined grimly that he would seek a closer acquaintance with his mysterious enemy.

But it was time to do something about these thugs. He glanced at his watch. Ten o'clock. Only an hour since he had been sitting beside Nita in the Drama Theatre. Then, they had looked forward to a future of peace, of happiness with each other. And in a trice all that had been changed.

Now, peril loomed for Nita, and the compelling mystery of Rodman's death, of Mrs. Sabin's telegram, lay between Wentworth and Nita. Mephisto had promised that the next attack would be through Nita. Wentworth believed that. The man must have great stakes involved, in whatever murderous game he was playing. And he was resourceful. The very carefulness with which this attack had been planned was an indication of the man's resourcefulness. If it failed, it would only be through their ignorance of the fact that Wentworth knew all his own employees. Had Wentworth been only a tenant in the building, as Mephisto must have supposed, he might not have questioned the presence of the alien operator, might have come up here to walk into the guns of these four.

Now, however, the position was to be reversed. These thugs were to be surprised. But even at that, the odds were with them—four to one. Wentworth did not intend to invoke the aid of the police. He purposed to go to Midwest City tonight, and he did not want to be detained for questioning. Neither did he intend to use the assistance of any of the service men in the building. He did not want them injured or killed.

HE HUNCHED forward his shoulders to bring the twin holster clear for a quick draw, and opened the door of the apartment, stepped out on the terrace. He had all four figures in view, and he saw how they swung about, startled, at the sound of the slamming door behind him.

And before they could grasp the fact that their man was here, his hands had streaked up and down from his shoulder holsters, and were gripping the butts of the two heavy automatics.

"Stand still!" he commanded tersely.

For a moment that tableau was still, immovable. Wentworth could plainly see the man whom the doorman had mistaken for himself. He stood near the parapet, and was clothed in a gray business suit. He was of the same build as Wentworth, and he carried himself somewhat the same. A little clever make-up would easily have deceived the doorman in the dark.

Now, one of the thugs cursed, and shouted to the others. "Hell! He's alone! Let's take him!"

Wentworth was prepared for that. In fact, he had hoped that they would resist. One of the figures moved, sprang to one side, and fired. The shot slapped the air alongside Wentworth's head, ricocheted off the steel door behind him. Now all four of the thugs sprang into motion, spreading out across the lawn. Their guns spat flame from different spots.

And Richard Wentworth, disdaining to move from his position, disdaining to take cover, traded shots with them. His twin automatics spoke almost as one gun, his shots speeding accurately, fired with the careful deliberation of the trained fighter. Just so had the Spider always fought against odds—in the open, relying on his uncanny skill with firearms to carry him through.

That skill did not fail him now. His slugs searched out those shadowy figures, caught one squarely between the eyes, the second through the heart. The third was firing from behind the protection of one of the umbrella trees, and Wentworth could see only the edge of one shoulder. He fired once, saw the shoulder jerk under the impact of the heavy slug, saw the man stagger, collapse to the lawn.

Wentworth swung around in search of the fourth man. That last one was the man who had been disguised to resemble him. The fellow must have taken shelter somewhere on the lawn. He must have emptied his gun at Wentworth, and must be even now frantically reloading it.

The echoes of the crashing gunfire were drifting away as Wentworth leaped off the terrace on to the lawn, crouched, with his guns ready, tautly listening. He was not worried about the sounds of the shooting. The walls and roof of this building were thoroughly soundproofed, and the tenants would hear only a faint echo of the firing.

The wounded man behind the umbrella tree groaned, then there was silence. And in that silence, Wentworth distinctly heard the click of a shell being ejected from a gun. His double was reloading.

The sound had come from the shadows close to the parapet. Wentworth could have fired at that sound. But he knew it would take the fellow several seconds to get the cartridges into the chamber, and to snap the chamber back into place. So instead of shooting, he launched himself across the lawn in a swift sprint that carried him close to the parapet.

And then he sighted the figure of his double, saw the man bending desperately over his gun. The fellow was not finished loading. He turned to run.

Wentworth holstered both automatics, leaped at the running man in a low flying tackle that caught him around the knees, brought him down with a thud.

The man was strong, wiry. His arms locked about Wentworth's waist, and he twisted, thrashed about on the ground, trying to get on top of Wentworth.

Wentworth smashed at the side of his head with a bunched fist. He missed, caught the man on the ear. The fellow gasped, let go his grip, and scrambled to his feet, clubbing his revolver for a blow.

Wentworth came up with him, both fists pistoning in and out

45

with the rapidity of a pneumatic drill. The other tried to cover up but Wentworth bored in, driving him backward, back toward the parapet. The fellow suddenly realized the danger behind him, and fought desperately.

Suddenly, the man raised his voice, shouted: "For God's sake, Lorsch, give it to him!"

Wentworth knew what that meant. Lorsch must be the man he had wounded. The fellow must have picked up his gun again, and would shoot as soon as he had the opportunity.

Alert to the new menace behind him, Wentworth began to weave from side to side as he fought, so as to make his back a more difficult target for Lorsch. His fists pistoned in and out, smashing into his antagonist's face. From behind him he heard Lorsch shout: "Hold him still, Kryle. Here goes!"

With a lightening sidestep, Wentworth smashed home a stinging uppercut against Kryle's jaw, sent him backward against the low parapet. Kryle uttered a scream, clawed the air, trying to keep himself from going over into space. At the same instant, a shot belched from behind Wentworth.

Wentworth literally felt the bullet singe his coat sleeve as it shrieked past, to bury itself in Kryle's chest.

Kryle hurled backward, screaming. His feet left the ground, and his body balanced for a split instant on the top of the parapet, then toppled over!

Wentworth shuddered. There was nothing between the roof and the ground below. Kryle would fall sixteen stories, into the narrow alley at the side of the building!

Wentworth swung around, crouched, while at the same time

his right hand flicked up, drew the automatic from his left shoulder holster. Lorsch fired again and the bullet chipped brick from the parapet.

Wentworth coolly shot once, a little to the right of the flash of Lorsch's gun. The bellow of his own automatic mingled with the explosion of Lorsch's next shot, which went wild. Then Lorsch's body crashed to the lawn, twitched and lay still. He was shot through the heart!

Wentworth did not spare him a second glance, but turned and leaned over the parapet, staring down into the blackness of the alley below. Kryle's body would be down there, smashed to a pulp, unrecognizable.

Unrecognizable!

The word suddenly thundered in Wentworth's brain. And he knew in a flash what he must do—what he must do in order to keep the girl he loved safe from Professor Mephisto, while the Spider walked again!

CHAPTER 4
"WENTWORTH IS DEAD!"

S WIFTLY, HE set to work. He went to each of the dead thugs in turn, and searched their clothing thoroughly— being careful not to disturb the guns they had held in their hands when they died. He took nothing from them, but examined all papers carefully. In the right hand coat pocket of the man, Lorsch, he found a match book. Upon the inside cover of the book was written a single telephone number: Hastings 2-4037.

He found that same number jotted down on the back of a card in the pocket of the second, and on the margin torn from a newspaper in the pocket of the third. That telephone number was the only thing common to all of them. He wrote it down in his own note book, then hurried into the apartment, leaving the bodies just where they had fallen.

Inside, he got himself two fresh automatics, but still retained the two he had used in the battle. From a wall safe he took out five thousand dollars in currency—four thousand-dollar bills, nine hundreds, and a hundred in smaller denominations. He might need large sums of money in Midwest City, before he was through. The last thing he took was a needle and thread from a darning set in Jenkyns' room. Then he made his way to the rear, and used the secret elevator to descend to the basement. He still carried the small package containing the Spider's cloak and hat.

He left the basement, being careful that the service men in the front should not observe him, and stole into the alley alongside. In the dark he stooped beside the crushed, pulpy mass that had been Kryle.

He flicked on his pencil flashlight, and felt a momentary spasm of nausea at sight of the gruesome remains. He forced himself to go through Kryle's pockets, removing every paper and bit of identification. It was bloody work, for Kryle had struck the side of the adjoining building with his head, and his skull was caved in. Blood and gory bits of human body clung to the man's clothing, but Wentworth forced himself to go on. He pocketed Kryle's driving license, a card case, a memo book which he saw contained the Hastings telephone number, and an assorted lot of knickknacks.

Then he transferred into Kryle's pockets all of his own identifying possessions. He gave the dead man his own card case containing licenses and club membership cards, his own keys, and his fountain pen and pencil. He added his wallet after he had shifted the five thousand dollars, which he had removed from the wall safe, into his own inside coat pocket.

Then he laid his two hot automatics alongside the body, and went around flashing the light in search of Kryle's gun. He found it twenty feet from the body, where it had fallen, and pocketed it.

Then he proceeded to the next step. From the inside of his own coat he cut the tailor's label. It was the label of one of the most fashionable men's tailoring establishments on Fifth Avenue. He cut the label from Kryle's coat, and sewed his own into it, using the needle and thread with which he had provided himself.

The whole operation took him at least a half hour. He worked cautiously, fearful that someone passing in the street might spot the tiny beam of his flashlight. He also had to be careful not to get any of the blood on his hands or clothing.

At last he stood up, finished. To all intents and purposes, Richard Wentworth lay there, crushed and broken, with a bullet-hole in his chest that had been fired from the revolver of one of the dead thugs upstairs on the roof. The police would have no difficulty in reconstructing the crime as he intended they should; Wentworth had been attacked on the roof, had engaged in a

gun fight with his assailants, and had succeeded in killing all of them. But he himself had been hit, had toppled over the parapet.

Richard Wentworth was dead. And when the Spider was later heard from in Midwest City, Professor Mephisto would believe himself mistaken. It would prove to Mephisto that Wentworth had not been the Spider, and he would assume that he could gain nothing by harassing Nita van Sloan. And while he awaited a report from the surviving member of the gang, Wentworth would be speeding west—a living ghost!

Silently, Wentworth stole out of the alley, hurried to the corner, and hailed a cab. It was ten-twenty as he instructed the driver to go to the Pennsylvania Station....

Kyle uttered a scream, clawed the air. A shot rang out behind Wentworth.

HE HAD instructed Jack Lawson to wait for him at the information booth at the Pennsylvania Station. But instead of going to meet the literary agent, Wentworth went into a booth and phoned the Coast Hotel.

"Let me talk to Mr. Sanders, who has just registered there," he said. Then, when he got Laskar: "Ben! Any reports?"

"Yes, boss. I called Fogarty's Detective Agency, and he's put a dozen men on the job. They've been phoning in direct to me. They've got a tail on Jack Lawson at the Pennsylvania Station. He's waiting at the information booth for you. And another Fogarty man just called to say that he's been on the tail of Mr. Blakely. Blakely and his wife just left their home—and where do you think they went?"

"Pennsylvania Station!" Wentworth guessed.

"Wrong this time, boss," Laskar chuckled. "They drove out to Newark Airport. They chartered a plane there, and they took off five minutes ago—for Midwest City! The Fogarty man wants to know should he follow on another plane."

"Never mind," Wentworth instructed. "Keep the shadows on Alma Rodman, and push your inquiries about the Mongols. I'm leaving for Midwest City at eleven. If you read anything about my death in the newspapers disregard it—it'll be greatly exaggerated. And remember, not a word to Miss van Sloan, or Ram Singh, or Jackson, as to where I am!"

He hung up, but did not go to the information booth. Instead, he went downstairs to the men's comfort room. Here he chose one of the individual cubicles, equipped with running water, where travelers can wash up and change their clothes.

He had only about five minutes before the train pulled out, and he worked fast. Opening his make-up case, he swiftly and expertly applied plastic material and pigment—little touches here and there that changed the cast of his countenance. He inserted two little platinum plates into his nostrils, which had the effect of broadening his nose. A touch of pigment thickened his eyebrows. A few more touches, and his work was complete. When he left the comfort booth, no one would have, recognized him as Richard Wentworth.

He hurried upstairs, bought a ticket for Midwest City, and saw Jack Lawson fidgeting impatiently at the information booth. Hawkins was glancing at the clock. It was one minute of eleven. The agent seemed to be undecided what to do, then shrugged, started away.

Wentworth followed him, saw him enter the train gate. He had evidently decided to go alone rather than miss the train. Wentworth entered directly behind him, and found that his berth was in the same car as that of Lawson. The berths were all made up, and Wentworth had no chance to try to spot the Fogarty man who would be tailing the agent. In any event, it did not matter, because he did not intend to disclose himself to anyone. With the exception of Laskar, the world must believe Richard Wentworth dead!

Lawson passed him in the aisle, gave him a casual glance, but failed to recognize him. Wentworth smiled in satisfaction. He did not actively suspect Jack Lawson of having any complicity in the death of Rodman—Lawson stood to gain much more with the playwright alive. Yet he did not entirely trust the man.

It would be safer for Lawson also to think that Wentworth was dead.

He got into his berth, undressed, and went to sleep at once. It was a peculiar characteristic of Richard Wentworth that he could push everything from his mind at a given time, and drop off to sleep without delay. It was the way he kept his mind fresh. When he awoke in the morning, he would immediately be ready to tackle the problem of Rodman's death, and the urgent telegram of Mrs. Norman Sabin.

There was no room in his mind for what he called "that useless mental activity which is known as "worry." People, he would say, are too prone to revolve and revolve some certain problem in their minds, thinking around it for hours, arriving nowhere, but wearing themselves out in the process. They will think about it while eating, walking, working, and even—subconsciously—while sleeping. Such constant attention to a given problem dulls and tires the brain, so that when the time actually comes to meet it, the mind is physically weak. That process is worry.

Wentworth never actually worried, for he had long ago learned that one must keep one's mind fresh and keen in a contest with any antagonist. So when he lay down in that berth, he dropped off to sleep at once, in spite of the desperate battle he had fought on the roof of his apartment house, in spite of the gruesome work he had been compelled to do in order to plant his own identity on the body of a dead man, and in spite of the dozen little but unanswerable questions that were already injecting themselves into the so-called suicide of Selden Rodman—questions which had already convinced him that Professor Mephisto was no ordinary, petty criminal, but a dangerous man of far-reaching power and no conscience.

He was convinced that the conclusive struggle with Mephisto would take place in Midwest City. In Midwest City, the Spider would meet a powerful antagonist—an antagonist who fought with no ordinary weapons, and whose evil motive was still clouded in mystery. It was with an added tang of exhilaration that Wentworth dropped off to sleep. He could enjoy to the full the coming battle, especially since he felt that Nita van Sloan would be safe in New York....

IN BUSTLING Midwest City the following day, a strange figure paced the floor of a semi-darkened room. The man was stocky, powerfully built; but of his face nothing could be seen, because of the startlingly different headgear which he wore.

Upon his head rested the sort of helmet which the Knights Templar of old might have worn in the Crusades. It was fashioned of steel at the top, while ripping chain-mail of fine-woven mesh hung from the sides and back, protecting the back of his head and neck. In front, too, another strip of meshed chain-mail was connected with the mesh at the sides, so that his entire face, except for the eyes, was hidden from view.

Those eyes flashed with a peculiar sort of glittering fire as he paced quickly up and down. Long gauntlets were drawn upon his hands, and strapped at the wrists. Otherwise, he was dressed in conventional business costume. The contrast between the medieval helmet and the modern clothes was startling.

A slant-eyed Mongol had just entered this room, and was handing the helmeted one a newspaper. He took it, brusquely waved the Mongol out, then glanced down at the headlines. A soft sigh of triumph escaped from behind the meshed chain-mail.

The headlines read:

NOTED CLUBMAN MURDERED
Richard Wentworth, Wealthy Sportsman,
Found Crushed to Death
After 16-Story Fall

The evidence of a battle to the death was discovered early this morning at the home of Richard Wentworth, whose name has often appeared in headline news. He was noted as an adventurous explorer and sportsman, as well as an inveterate seeker after danger, having fought in many wars and in many lands as a volunteer. He fought his last battle late last evening, on the lawn in front of his penthouse apartment, against great odds. And as the police reconstruct his death, he put up a good fight. Three of his assailants were found dead....

The helmeted man continued to read avidly, calling out: "Come in!" in an annoyed voice when someone rapped on the door.

The person who entered now was even more arresting in appearance than the helmeted man. He was a slant-eyed Mongol, but he was not dressed in the Western clothes worn by those who had attacked Wentworth in New York. He wore wide pantaloons, and a scarlet jacket, open all the way down the front, to reveal numerous hideous figures painted or tattooed upon his chest. He wore a moustache whose ends hung down past his chin, and upon his head was a curious peaked helmet with a sort of pyramid point, and a trimming of small trinkets which upon closer examination turned out to be dried-up and shrunken human ears.

This revoltingly ugly man raised a hand to the other in salute, and addressed him in a deep, rumbling voice, speaking in English with a guttural accent.

"You have summoned the Mongol Shaman to council. I am here. Speak your thoughts, Professor Mephisto!"

Mephisto's voice emanated from behind the chain-mail, sounding soft and feeble by contrast with that of the Mongol. But there was another quality in that voice—a quality of silken cruelty—that caused even the Mongol to look at him respectfully.

"I have summoned you here, Akbar the Cunning, to tell you the good news. The one man whose interference I feared is dead. Here is the report. The Spider need no longer be feared."

Akbar the Cunning smiled. "It is good."

Mephisto went on. "Now we can proceed with our other plans. With the Rodman matter closed, we can turn to the next man—Paul Tilson. Do you think your Mongols will obey you if you order them to seize Tilson's wife and child?"

Akbar drew himself up. "Am I not the Mongol Shaman—the High Priest of all the Buriat Mongols? I have influence over all the spirits of good and of evil. They will obey me, or I will set the evil spirits upon them!"

Mephisto's voice was slightly amused. "You know very well

you're only a faker, Akbar. You have the Mongols fooled, and they fall for you. I wonder if they will not discover you are a fraud, if you push them too hard."

"They will discover nothing!" The Mongol Shaman spoke scornfully. "For three thousand years the Buriat Mongols have followed their Shamans blindly, with faith. They will obey me now. What do you wish done?"

"I want this done. Paul Tilson is recalcitrant. He thinks he can defy me. Tilson runs a chain of food stores, and it would ruin him to raise the money which I require from him. But he must be made to do it—scared into doing it. You will assign three of your men to the task. They will break into his home, seize his wife and child, and bring them to the Pit. They will leave this card where Tilson can find it."

He picked up a card from his desk, handed it to the Mongol Shaman. It was a small card, some three inches by five. It was all black; and painted upon it in glaring red was a strange symbol—the three balls which have come to be known as the pawnbroker's sign!

Beneath the sign of the three balls the following message was lettered, also in red:

Paul Tilson—

Your wife and child are in pawn to Mephisto. You know the price required to redeem them—and you know the price they will pay if you fail!

There was no signature on the card—only that.

The Mongol Shaman took it, glanced at it, and raised his eyebrows. "It shall be done, Professor Mephisto—today."

He turned, stalked from the room. At the door he stopped a moment, looked back at the helmeted man, then glanced down at the three balls on the card. He smiled sardonically.

"Mephisto!" he exclaimed. "I have a better name—*The Devil's Pawnbroker!*" He twirled the ends of his long moustache, and winked.

Mephisto laughed. "Pawnbroker, indeed," he said softly. "Pawnbroker in lives!"

CHAPTER 5
THE SPIDER STRIKES

WENTWORTH'S TRAIN had arrived in Midwest City at eleven in the morning. His first act was to phone Mrs. Norman Sabin, at 222 North Alameda Drive—the address she had given in her telegram.

There was no answer.

He went from the station to the Alameda Hotel, and registered as William Worth.

"Room 1408 is a light, airy room," the clerk told him. "I'm sure you'll like it. Do you intend to stay long, sir?"

"I don't know yet. Maybe a day, maybe a week—maybe forever." He looked around the busy lobby. "I hear you had a little excitement here yesterday."

The clerk looked embarrassed. "Yes, sir. It was very unfortunate. I saw it all. Mr. Rodman stood up in the center of the lobby—right there, next to the fern, sir—and deliberately raised the gun to his temple. I shouted to him to stop, but he laughed horribly, and pulled the trigger!"

Wentworth raised his eyebrows. "Seems strange, doesn't it? His play was successful."

"Yes, sir, that's true. He got a telegram from his New York agent, only ten minutes earlier. I handed him the telegram, and he read it right here at the desk. I noted at the time that he didn't look quite right, and he just crushed the telegram and threw it in the wastepaper basket. Then he went to the phones, and made two calls. And not ten minutes later, he committed suicide!"

"How do you know the telegram was from his New York agent?" Wentworth asked.

The clerk smiled knowingly. "After he shot himself, I thought of that telegram, and picked it out of the basket. I gave it to the police, of course, but I remember just what it contained. It went something like this: 'Drums of Desire going over great stop you have nothing to worry about for the rest of your life stop now you can get yourself out of hock.' And it was signed, Jack Lawson."

Wentworth's brow wrinkled. "You're sure it said 'Now you can get yourself out of hock?'"

"That's right, sir. I guess it meant he was in debt—"

"I see," Wentworth said absently. "And you say he made *two* phone calls after that?"

"Exactly."

"Thanks. Very interesting." Wentworth took his key. "Never mind calling a bellboy. I don't think I'll go up at once."

He left the desk, went over to the railed-off section where the telephones were located. There were a dozen booths, with a switchboard operator, for the convenience of guests. Wentworth waited until the operator was free, then he asked her: "Were you on duty here last night when Mr. Rodman committed suicide?"

The girl glanced at him annoyedly. "Yes, I was. And I'm tired of answering questions about it."

"Maybe this will make you feel better," Wentworth told her. He slipped a twenty-dollar bill into her hand.

She smiled. "Well, it doesn't exactly make me feel bad. What did you want to know?"

"Rodman made two calls before he committed suicide. What were the numbers he called?"

She flipped back the pages of her call book, put her finger on two numbers. "Here they are, mister. I'm not supposed to do this, you know."

Wentworth didn't answer her. He was busy jotting down the numbers. One of them was Alameda 4-3681. The other was one he already had—Hastings 2-4037!

Hastings 2-4037—the number he had found in the pockets of each of those killers back in New York!

HE THANKED the girl, and hurried across the lobby to a row of public phone booths. He didn't want the operator to listen in on the calls he was making. He called the telephone company, and asked for the names and addresses of the subscribers at those two numbers. Though it was against the rules of the telephone company to divulge such information, he got it by giving the name of a certain friend of his who was employed by the Department of Justice. He very seldom made use of the name of Jerry Tilden, but he needed that information quickly now.

He learned that Alameda 4-3681 was the number of a Mr. Paul Tilson, at 416 North Cort-landt Avenue. The name meant nothing to him, but to be on the safe side he wired Laskar in New York to hire a Midwest City detective to look the man up, and shadow him. As for the Hastings number, he was told that it was a public telephone booth in a cigar store at 221 North Alameda Avenue.

He left the phone booth thoughtfully. Mrs. Sabin's address was 222 North Alameda, only a few doors down from this hotel. That would mean that the cigar store was directly opposite the residence of Mrs. Sabin. Each one of those killers had the cigar store number jotted down. That could mean only one thing—that it was the number they called to get in touch with some superior—perhaps Professor Mephisto.

No doubt, Mephisto had some third person at that phone, to transmit messages and take them to him. The professor would be too clever to leave an open link between himself and those gunmen.

He left the hotel, walked down Alameda Drive. This was a sort of mixed business and residential street. Midwest City had grown fast, and swanky apartment houses adjoined hotels and business places. For instance, on this block stood the Alameda Hotel, then a small department store, and on the corner was number 222, where Mrs. Sabin lived. Opposite, the cigar store at 221 was one of a row of one-story taxpayers.

The cross street here was North Cortlandt Avenue, and from the way the numbers ran, Wentworth judged that the home of Paul Tilson would be down the middle of the next block.

He went into the cigar store, bought a package of cigarettes, and noted that there was a pool room in the rear, where the public phone was located.

Two or three of the pool tables were in use, and several men loitered around, watching the games. There was an "out-of-order sign" on the telephone.

Wentworth's eyes narrowed. He took a nickel out of his pocket, stepped up to the instrument. He noted swiftly that its number was Hastings 2-4037. He started to insert the nickel in the slot, when a gruff voice behind him called out: "Hey! Don't you see the sign? That phone is out of order!"

Wentworth turned to see a stocky, square-jawed chap at one of the tables waving to him with his cue. "Whatsa-matter?" the square-jawed one demanded. "Can't you read?"

Wentworth smiled sheepishly, looking at the sign. "I guess I didn't notice it. Thanks for saving me a nickel."

The square-jawed chap grunted, and went back to his pool game.

Wentworth left the cigar store, and crossed the street toward Mrs. Sabin's house. The names in the mail boxes showed him that the Sabin apartment was on the fifth floor. There was a self-service elevator, but he did not go up. He rang the bell, waited, then rang again. There was no answer.

It was peculiar that Mrs. Sabin should not be home after having sent the telegram of appeal to the Spider. Wentworth did not go up to investigate. Instead, he walked around the corner, and found number 416 North Cortlandt, where Paul Tilson lived. This was the second call that Selden Rodman had made. Wentworth wanted to find what connection there was between Tilson and Rodman.

Number 416 was an apartment house, similar to the one in which the Sabins lived. As he approached the building, he saw three men emerge from it, with a girl of about seven. Two of the men were gripping the girl tightly, hurrying her toward a car parked at the curb, while the third rushed ahead of them to open the door.

Wentworth thrilled as he recognized the Oriental features of those men. They were Mongols, like the men who had attacked him yesterday at the Drama Theatre!

THE LITTLE girl was struggling with her captors, trying to cry out. No sound came, however, for one of the Mongols had his hand over her mouth.

Wentworth's eyes became cold and bleak. His hand slid to and from his shoulder holster, just as the three Mongols reached the car with the child. He leveled his gun, taking careful aim, for he did not want to hit the little girl. But he never fired.

Just at that moment, a smashing blow cracked down upon his arm, and a voice shouted almost in his ear: "Drop that gun!"

He swung, to face an angry patrolman. The bluecoat had

He stooped beside the body to feel for a pulse.

struck at Wentworth's arm with his nightstick, and now he sought to grapple with Wentworth. "A gunman, huh!" he growled.

Wentworth's arm was numbed, but he gripped the patrolman's sleeve with his left hand. "You idiot! Don't you see that's a kidnapping? Good God! You've helped the kidnappers to escape!"

The patrolman frowned, glanced toward the spot where the three Mongols had been with the girl. They were all in the car now, and as it started away, they saw the child's hands waving frantically out of the rear window. A single shriek, and then silence. The car sped away.

The patrolman exclaimed: "My Gawd! A snatch!" He clawed frantically for his revolver, saying to Wentworth: "Gawd, I'm sorry, mister. I thought *you* was the gunman!"

Wentworth snapped up his automatic, sent a single shot screaming after the auto. But it was already turning the far corner, and it disappeared just as he fired.

The patrolman started to run after the car, waving his gun and shouting. Wentworth shrugged. It would be useless to try to follow that car now. He let the patrolman go, and hurried into number 416, while the pedestrians out in the street took up the shouts of the patrolman. There would be an alarm out for that auto at once, but Wentworth was almost sure that it would not be picked up. If those Mongols were agents of Professor Mephisto, the kidnapping must have been carefully planned. They would be certain to have at their command an effective means of throwing off pursuit.

The lobby of number 416 was quiet, as if nothing had happened here. There was no one about. Apparently those men had kidnapped the child without arousing the building.

Wentworth looked in the letter boxes, found that Tilson's apartment was on the third floor—3F. Somehow, he had a feeling that he would learn more about that kidnapping from the Tilson apartment. Those Mongols were certainly connected somehow with the suicide of Rodman. Rodman had called Tilson.

Wentworth took the self-service elevator up to the third, and found the door of 3F. He tried the knob, found it unlocked. He pushed the door open, found himself looking into one of those two-room-and-kitchenette apartments that are so common in the modern, more expensive apartment buildings.

The thing that attracted his eye was the body of the woman, lying in the middle of the floor. She was on her face, and there was no question about whether she was dead. The handle of a long, ugly knife protruded from between her shoulder blades. **WENTWORTH SWORE** under his breath. This woman must have died defending the child who had just been kidnapped. Whether she was the child's mother or nurse, he did not know.

He had been careful to open the door as noiselessly as possible. And now, as he stood just outside the foyer, gazing into the living room, he became aware of stealthy movement somewhere in the apartment.

Someone was in there with the dead woman!

Wentworth's eyes narrowed. The kidnappers must have left

one or more of their number behind for some purpose. Was it to search the apartment, or to lie in wait for anyone else? Only a fool or a reckless fanatic would have remained in there after a kidnapping. From what he had seen of these Mongols, he understood that they must be acting under the orders of someone whom they feared even more than the law of this strange Western country to which they had been brought.

His eyes spotted a small card lying beside the dead body. He determined to enter the apartment, in spite of the fact that he was sure someone was in there. But he dared not show himself as he was now. He intended to carry on a number of inquiries in Midwest City, and if he were spotted by the enemy, his usefulness would be over. Swiftly he withdrew from under his coat the small flat bundle which he had carried with him. He shook out the wide cape and the broad-brimmed hat of the Spider, and donned them.

As he worked, he heard the continued sounds of stealthy movement inside, but whoever was there must be in an adjoining room, for he was invisible to Wentworth from the doorway.

Wentworth removed his make-up case from an inner pocket, and swiftly applied the plastic material, the pigment and the false teeth which he used when he appeared as the Spider. He was so used to this make-up that he hardly needed a mirror. In two minutes he was finished. The Spider stood in that doorway!

Wentworth rattled the knob of the door to give warning to whoever was in there, then stepped boldly into the room, and knelt beside the dead woman. He was conscious of a quickly indrawn breath somewhere behind him. As he entered the

room he had noted out of the
corner of his eye that there was
a kitchenette arrangement at
one side of the room, hidden
by a wide curtain. He knew
now that the marauder in that
apartment was in the kitchenette.

With all his senses keyed up
to the highest point of alert-
ness, he stooped beside the body, felt for a pulse. The woman
was dead. Blood from the wound in her back had stained her
dress, and was congealing on her white skin. He did not touch
the knife, but carefully picked up the card that was lying beside
her. He did this with his left hand, keeping his right free, and
close to his shoulder holster.

His eyes narrowed as he scanned the card. A light of triumph
appeared in them. This brought him much closer to an intelli-
gent idea of the purpose of Professor Mephisto. At the top of
the card was the insignia of the three balls. The message was the
one that Mephisto had prepared for Paul Tilson:

> Your wife and child are in pawn to Mephisto. You know the
> price required to redeem them—and you know the price they
> will pay if you fail!

Now, however, the words "your wife and child are" had been
changed in pencil to "Your child is," and the word "them" had
been changed to "her."

It was apparent to Wentworth from this that the original plan had been to kidnap both, but that the mother had resisted, and been killed.

HE WAS thinking of this message with only half his mind. With the other half he was waiting for the attack from behind which he was sure would come. He was reasonably certain that whoever was in this apartment would not use a gun, for fear of attracting police. They would not expect police to come up to this apartment, even if the kidnappers were seen escaping, for there would be nothing to show from which apartment they had come. Therefore, the marauder in the kitchenette would not deliberately do anything to give the alarm. In addition, this card had been left for Tilson, and no one else to find. The answer was that the man hiding in the kitchenette would use a knife or a bludgeon.

And Wentworth was not disappointed. His keen ears caught the faint sound of a swishing curtain, the quick pad of feet, a hissing intake of breath.

He twisted to the left, and glimpsed the snarling Mongol, who had launched himself through the air at his back, gripping a gleaming knife. Had he not turned at that instant, he would have been found beside the woman, with a knife between his shoulder blades, just like her.

But his quick action saved his life. The Mongol, seeing that he was discovered, tried to swing his blade for Wentworth's face. Wentworth's gun had leaped into his hand as he moved to the left, and now he pulled the trigger once. The shot blasted squarely in the Mongol's chest, the heavy-caliber slug crashing through his breast-bone as if it had been *papier-mâché*.

The man screamed once, and seemed to have been pushed backward by a powerful hand. His body appeared to be suspended in the air for an instant, and then collapsed, while blood poured from his chest in a geyser-like flow. He lay beside the dead woman, on his back, gasping out his life, then suddenly was convulsed in the agony of death. He stiffened and died, while Wentworth watched him without mercy.

Then the Spider moved into swift action. The reverberations of his gunshot were still drumming against the walls of the room, and someone was shouting downstairs. The Spider drew from his pocket a small platinum cigarette lighter, snapped open a secret compartment at the bottom. He pressed the open bottom of the lighter against the forehead of the dead Mongol.

When he stood up, there appeared upon the Mongol's forehead a livid design—the figure of a spider! It was the Spider's trademark, known throughout the underworld. Whenever a criminal was found with the mark upon his forehead, the underworld knew that the Spider had exacted a vengeance that the law had failed to exact.

The Spider smiled grimly. Professor Mephisto would know, now, that he had not eliminated the Spider!

People were shouting in the corridor, and he knew that they would be in here in a moment. He stooped, picked up the card beside the woman, and hurried through into the next room. There was an open window, and a fire escape here. The Spider was out that window in a trice, and running down the fire escape ladder, even before the police began pounding at the apartment door above.

And when the police finally broke in the door, crashed into the apartment, they heard a weird, blood-chilling laugh from somewhere outside. They gazed at each other, then at the livid mark on the forehead of the Mongol.

"The Spider!" they whispered, with awe in their eyes. "The Spider's in Midwest City!"

CHAPTER 6
PITCHED BATTLE

IT WAS growing dark as Wentworth made his way out through the alley in which he had found himself. He had removed his cape and hat, and his Spider make-up, and he sauntered down Alameda Drive, his mind working swiftly, in sharp contrast to his outward casual appearance.

Somewhere in this city was located the headquarters of Professor Mephisto. In that headquarters would be the child of Paul Tilson, who had just been kidnapped. In that headquarters would also be the answer to the suicide of Selden Rodman.

That this was more than an ordinary kidnapping racket, he was convinced. No kidnapper would have acted so boldly; no kidnapper would have left so cryptic a note as the one that Wentworth now carried in his pocket.

From the wording of the note, it was apparent that Tilson must have had dealings with Mephisto, in the past. If Tilson could be located before he was apprised of the death of his wife and the kidnapping of his child, he might be made to divulge what he knew. And it was fairly certain that what he knew might throw some light on Rodman's suicide.

Several courses were open to the Spider now. He could follow up the Tilson lead, or he could try to interview Mrs. Sabin, or he could try to locate the headquarters of Mephisto through the square-jawed thug in the pool room.

The police would be working on the Tilson case now, of course. But Wentworth was convinced that Mephisto did not fear the police. That man of evil had some hold on his victims that prevented them from invoking the help of the law.

Wentworth returned to the Alameda Hotel, and put in a long distance call for Laskar, at the Coast Hotel in New York. Laskar's report was disturbing and mystifying. The Fogarty operative who had followed Jack Lawson to Midwest City on the same train with Wentworth had phoned by long distance. Lawson had registered at the Alameda Hotel, had gone to the morgue to view the body of Rodman, and had then made a call upon a Mrs. Sabin at 222 North Alameda Drive. The two had gone out, and were even now dining at the Alameda Hotel restaurant.

As for Thomas Blakely, the president of the Orient Insurance Company, Fogarty had wired an agency in Midwest City with whom he often worked, and that agency had placed an operative at the airport where Blakely's chartered plane was due to arrive. He had picked up Blakely and his wife at the airport, had followed them into Midwest City, and had lost them in traffic.

THOMAS BLAKELY

JACK LAWSON

DR. NORMAN SABIN

74

They did not know where the Orient Life Insurance Company president had gone.

"What about the Mongols?" Wentworth asked. "Did you dig anything up on them?"

"I did, boss. I got the dope at Ellis Island. There were twenty-three of them came in within the last two months. They entered on six-month permits, and their bonds were furnished by a party named Akbar Azakan, of 221 North Alameda Drive, right there in Midwest City!"

Wentworth's eyes narrowed. That was the address of the pool room where he had seen the square-jawed thug. This was almost too good to be true. It proved without a shadow of doubt that the telephone number of that pool room was a direct connecting link with the headquarters of Mephisto.

"All right, Laskar. Good work so far. I'm registered at the Alameda Hotel here, as William Worth. When the Fogarty men phone in to you again, instruct them to contact me here. Call me if anything important arises."

He hung up, and went into the dining room. Sure enough, he spotted Jack Lawson, at a table near the window, immersed in conversation with a darkly beautiful woman who seemed to be under an exceptional strain of some kind.

At a nearby table, he spotted the Fogarty man who had been trailing Lawson. The woman with Lawson was undoubtedly Mrs. Sabin. That was why she had not been at home when Wentworth called.

WENTWORTH ALLOWED the headwaiter to lead him to a table close to theirs, and he ordered dinner. He watched

75

THE MONGOL SHAMAN

PAUL TILSON

ELSIE SABIN

Lawson and Mrs. Sabin while he ate. She was not more than thirty or thirty-one, he judged—rather young to be the wife of an eminently successful physician like Doctor Sabin. Her dress was cut daringly low, and she seemed to be full of vivacity and life, though her spirits appeared to be somewhat clouded over by some sort of trouble. To judge by the telegram of appeal she had sent to the Spider, there was plenty of reason for her to be worried.

Things seemed to be interlocking with puzzling exactitude in this case. Wentworth went over the main facts in his mind. Thomas Blakely had mentioned to him that the Orient Life was sustaining punishing losses through suicide claims. Mrs. Sabin feared that her husband, who was himself connected with the Orient Life, was about to commit suicide. Selden Rodman had actually taken his life, without apparent reason; and before doing so he had called a number demonstrated to be linked with Professor Mephisto. He had also called Paul Tilson, whose wife had just been killed, and whose child had been abducted by the agents of Mephisto. Thomas Blakely, the President of the Orient Life, had disappeared upon arriving at Midwest City. And Mrs. Sabin was here having dinner with the literary agent of the man who had committed suicide.

Apparently, every one of these people was in some way affected by the operations of Professor Mephisto. But Mephisto's connection with the losses sustained by the Orient Life was a problem that still remained a mystery.

Wentworth ate quickly, and was ready to leave at the same time as Jack Lawson and Mrs. Sabin. He followed them out into the street, saw them shake hands. Lawson went back into the hotel, and Mrs. Sabin walked down the street toward her apartment. Wentworth followed Mrs. Sabin. He knew that the Fogarty operative would keep Lawson under surveillance, and he wanted an interview with the wife of the physician.

He watched her enter her building, then worked around the block, seeking the back entrance. He had already scouted the building on his previous visits, and he knew just where he wanted to go. On the way past number 222, he glanced across at number 221, where the pool room and cigar store was located. And suddenly he stiffened.

A woman was sitting in a taxicab in front of that pool room, leaning forward in her seat in an attitude of anxiety. The street light fell across her face, so that Wentworth recognized her without difficulty.

That woman was Alma Rodman, the widow of Selden Rodman!

He had left her in New York yesterday, to be cared for by Nita van Sloan.

Wentworth did not break his stride, or indicate in any way that he had noticed her. Of course, she would not recognize him, due to the changes he had effected in his features; and there was little danger of her noticing anything now, for she seemed to be preoccupied and nervous.

Wentworth rounded the corner, saw an empty cab, and hailed it. "Park here," he ordered the driver, "and then follow that taxi in front of number 221 when it starts."

They waited for a couple of minutes, and then the door of

the cigar store opened. The square-jawed thug who had warned Wentworth away from the phone came out, looked around cautiously, then approached the cab. He opened the door, poked his head in, and exchanged a few words with Alma Rodman. Quickly she got out, paid off the driver, and waved him away.

Wentworth said to his own cabby: "Wait here. It's those two that I want to follow!"

Alma Rodman and the square-jawed thug waited at the curb for a moment, and almost at once a highly polished, well-kept limousine pulled up. Wentworth's blood raced as he noted that the driver of the limousine had the high cheek bones and the slant eyes of the Oriental. He was one of the Mongols!

Alma Rodman and her companion got into the limousine, and drove away.

"All right!" Wentworth rapped. "After them!"

THE LIMOUSINE rounded the corner into North Cortlandt, and Wentworth's cab followed at a safe distance. In the middle of the next block the chase ended. The limousine suddenly turned to the right, and pulled into an open air parking lot, set in between two rows of one-story taxpayers. There was a high fence around this parking lot, and a wooden gate which opened to permit the entrance of the limousine, then closed behind it at once.

A projecting sign on the door read:

OPEN AIR PARKING
10 Hours—$1.50

Wentworth's driver turned around in his seat. "What do you want me to do, mister?"

"Drive past," Wentworth instructed him, "and park at the curb. We'll wait till they come out."

Several minutes elapsed, and neither Alma Rodman nor the square-jawed thug appeared.

Wentworth said to his driver: "That's a pretty steep rate for parking, isn't it? Not many people could afford to pay $1.50 just to park for a few hours."

The cabby nodded. "It's funny about that joint, mister. It used to do a pretty good business up to a few months ago. They just charged twenty-five cents a day for parking—see? There's the old sign on the gate—and a lot of people used to leave their cars there when they came into town. But the joint was sold, and it looks like the new owner wants to keep it exclusive. He built the fence around it, and jacked up the rate. No one uses it any more. The guy must either be nuts, or he must have plenty of money."

Wentworth studied the place through the rear window. On either side of the parking lot were low-story stores, and the fence came up high enough so that it would be impossible to look into the lot from the roofs. Across the street, there were also nothing but one-story buildings, except for a single structure, directly opposite. That single structure was five floors in height, but appeared to be out of use. The windows were all boarded up, as well as the door.

Some sort of work was apparently being done upon this building in the daytime, for a painter's scaffold hung in front of the second story windows. A rope ladder hanging from the scaffold indicated how the painter ascended and descended.

"What is that building?" Wentworth asked.

"That used to be the old Midwest Brewery. They were closed all during prohibition, and then when repeal came in they started making beer. But the building inspectors found the building unsafe, and the Midwest Brewing people moved out to a more modern building out in the suburbs. This place was only sold a few weeks ago, and it looks like the new owner intends to remodel. They've had painters working on it for a month now, but they never seem to get farther than the second floor. I guess the owner ain't sure just what he's going to do with it."

Wentworth nodded thoughtfully.

Alma Rodman and the square-jawed fellow had not come out of the parking lot. This particular block had only the few stores on it, and apparently there was little business at night, for all the stores were closed. The street was virtually deserted, though North Alameda Drive, only a block away, was glittering with electric lights and throngs of people.

Wentworth decided to learn more about this parking lot. He got out of the cab, gave the driver a twenty-dollar bill. "I won't need you anymore," he said. "But you're a good man. What's your name?"

"John Grant, sir."

"All right, Grant. You work around the Alameda Hotel. I may have use for you later tonight. Keep your flag down. I'll pay for the waiting time."

Grant grinned. "That's a cinch job, mister. I'll be parked across the way from the Alameda."

Wentworth waited until the driver had left. He wanted a man like this to be ready for any emergency. The time might come when he would need fast transportation, and no questions asked. Grant would ask no questions, knowing that he paid well.

AS SOON as he was alone, Wentworth crossed the street toward the deserted brewery. He moved over into the shadow of an areaway at the side of the old building, and worked swiftly in the darkness, kneeling on the sidewalk. When he rose again, it was as the Spider. His dark cloak made of him no more than a shadow in the night, so that anyone passing would never have noticed him.

He moved slowly along the face of the building, under the scaffold, toward where the rope ladder hung down. He moved slowly, cautiously. To an observer, he would have seemed no more than a black splotch in the shadows.

Suddenly he stopped stock still. A car was coming slowly down the street. The headlights flooded the street, but did not touch the Spider. He stood immovable, his cloak high up over his face, while the car slowed up, then stopped at the curb before the entrance to the parking lot.

A man leaped out from this car, ran up to the gate, and pounded upon it with his fist.

Wentworth, watching from across the street, noted that a second car was crawling along down at the far end of the street, with its lights out. It was apparently shadowing the first, for it slowed down to a snail's pace, then came to a full stop about a hundred and fifty feet back.

In the meantime, the man who had alighted from the first car continued to pound against the gate. At last, a small wicket in the gate opened, and a voice in the quiet street asked: "What do you want?"

"I want my child!" the man shouted. "Damn you, you killed my wife. At least give me back my child—"

"Shut up, you fool!" the voice from behind the wicket snarled. "You want to bring the cops down? Where do you think you'd come off then?"

The man outside lowered his voice. "All right, all right. I'll do anything you say. Only for God's sake, don't harm my child!"

"Okay. Go away. We're busy now. Come back in two hours. You can see the boss then."

"And you won't harm my child in the meantime?"

"Naw. Not if you do like the boss wants you to!"

"All right. I'll do it!"

Wentworth tensed as he watched the man return to his car. This was Tilson, of course. The man seemed to be beside himself with grief and fear. But why, if he knew where the kidnapper's headquarters was, did he not bring the police? Wentworth wanted to talk to Tilson. But as Tilson drove away, he saw the car behind him pick up the trail. That would be one of the operatives whom Laskar had detailed to the job of shadowing Tilson. The operative would no doubt report to Mr. Worth at the Alameda Hotel. Wentworth would learn in that way where to find Tilson. In the meantime, he would investigate this parking lot.

Once more the street became quiet as the two cars pulled away.

The Spider moved ahead again, until he was directly beneath the rope ladder. He reached up, gripped the lowest rung, and raised himself, then swung a leg over, hoisted himself up, with his cape flapping behind him.

He reached the scaffold, clambered on to it, and stared across over the fence into the parking lot.

THERE WERE three cars in there. One was parked over against the wall, as if not in use. The limousine and another car were in the center of the lot, and several men stood about, two of them holding Alma Rodman on either side. One of them had a hand over her mouth. They had evidently kept her that way to prevent her crying out while Tilson was at the gate, and they had remained that way while one of their number peered through the wicket to make sure that he had left.

Now the lookout turned and waved to the others, and two of the men emerged from the second car, where they had apparently been hiding. Each of them carried a submachine gun.

Alma Rodman's two guards started to drag her forcibly toward the rear of the parking lot, where there was some kind of shed. One of the others got into the limousine, which had been jockeyed around to face toward the gate. The lookout stepped to the gate, slipped the latch, preparatory to opening it. It seemed that the limousine was going to leave again, after having brought Alma Rodman.

But Alma Rodman didn't want to go with the thugs. She began to struggle, and Wentworth could see her teeth sink into the hand of one of her captors. The man cursed and pulled away his hand, and Alma Rodman screamed.

One of the thugs struck her in the face, and her scream thinned into a wail of pain.

And just then, the driver of the limousine turned on his lights and started his motor. The glaring bright lights flashed over the fence, illuminating the front of the old brewery building, and sending light upward to bathe the cloaked and hatted figure on the scaffold.

Wentworth swiftly dropped, flattening himself against the scaffold. But it was too late. He had been spotted. And so well was he known to the underworld that he was immediately recognized.

One of the thugs shouted: "My Gawd! It's the Spider!"

Someone else shouted: "For Gawd's sake, give it to him quick, before he gets us!"

The two men with submachine guns raised their weapons, and their chattering began to fill the night air. Flashes of flame illuminated the parking space, and slugs whined through the air around the scaffold, gouged the wall of the brewery.

Wentworth was in action even before the machine guns began to sputter.

He was up on his feet, swaying with the scaffold, both automatics in his hands, the guns kicking and spitting death each time he pulled the trigger.

This was the figure that the underworld had learned to dread. Whenever the Spider stood thus, trading shots with his enemies, those enemies never walked again. Those two blazing automatics of the Spider had carried such terror to the underworld that a battle was half won when his automatics began to spit fire.

Now he shot coolly, calculatingly, making each slug tell, while the thugs spattered the front of the brewery with their wild lead.

And Alma Rodman took advantage of the diversion to turn and run toward the rear of the parking lot. The two thugs began to chase her, one of them snatching off her evening cloak.

At that moment Wentworth placed two careful shots in the headlights of the limousine, so that he was not such a glaring mark as he had been before.

He fired twice now, and downed both of the thugs who were chasing Alma Rodman. He did this before turning his attention to the machine gunners. But now the hail of lead from the submachine guns was coming uncomfortably close, as the thugs got the range.

The slugs were biting into the wood of the scaffold, traveling up toward Wentworth. He fired twice more, and as if miraculously, both machine guns ceased their chatter. The remaining thugs were frightened. They knew now that they had no chance against the Spider, and they turned to run, toward the back of the parking lot, in the direction taken by Alma Rodman.

Coolly, without mercy, Wentworth picked them off one after the other. Ordinarily he would not have shot at men who had ceased to fight; but he remembered the small child who had been kidnapped, remembered the poor dead woman with the knife in her back in the Tilson apartment. And he fired again and again. There was no one to follow Alma Rodman.

Now, police whistles were blowing, and sirens were screaming over on North Alameda. The police would be here at any moment.

Swiftly the Spider slipped fresh clips into his automatics, then climbed down the rope ladder from the scaffold and rushed across the street. The latch on the gate had been pulled, and the door opened to his touch. He entered the parking lot, his automatics thrust before him, his cloak flapping behind him.

He hurried past the dead bodies of the thugs, reached the rear of the lot, near the shed-like structure that he had noticed from the scaffold. There was no sign of Alma Rodman.

Wentworth circled the shed, found a locked door. There was no sign of life anywhere around. Mrs. Rodman had disappeared!

Wentworth's eyes were bleak as he made his way back toward the front of the parking lot. He could hear a police siren growing louder as it approached. Yet he paused for one task. On the forehead of each of those dead thugs he placed his seal—the livid reproduction of the Spider.

Here was notice to the whole world, and to the underworld in particular, that the Spider was fighting Mephisto. By tomorrow the word would be out in every dive and hot spot that the Spider was walking in Midwest City, and that his eye was as good as ever. Perhaps that would make it a little difficult for Mephisto to get new recruits to replace these casualties!

And then, like a wraith in the night, the Spider stole forth out of the parking lot, just as a police radio car rounded the far corner. His swirling cloak blended with the night, made him nothing more than a shadow among shadows. When the police arrived, they found nothing but dead men, with the seal of the Spider upon them.

And they shivered, as somewhere in the night there sounded the eerie, blood-chilling laughter of the Spider!

The battle was growing hotter. The Spider was in action!

CHAPTER 7
THE FRIGHTENED WOMAN

WENTWORTH DID not return at once to the Alameda Hotel. He stopped at 222 North Alameda Drive. He had been sidetracked from his purpose of interviewing Mrs. Sabin. The woman had sent an appeal to the Spider, and it was that as much as Selden Rodman's death which had brought him here to Midwest City.

He went around through the rear of the building, found the service elevator, which was out of use for the night.

He went up in this to Mrs. Sabin's floor. The service elevator let him out in a narrow hall, upon which faced the service doors of three apartments. Swiftly he donned his hat and cloak once more, produced his key case, and tried the door of the Sabin apartment. The latch offered only feeble resistance to his efforts, and in a moment he was ready to swing the door open.

He pushed it very cautiously, for a fraction of an inch, and noted that the room within was in darkness. He pushed it further open, stepped in, and closed it carefully behind him. He was in a dark kitchen, and through the swinging door opposite he could hear agitated voices in high-pitched conversation.

He stepped closer to the door, and immediately recognized the voice of Thomas Blakely, president of the Orient Life Insurance Company.

"I tell you, Sabin," Blakely was saying explosively, "the Orient Life can't stand many more of these losses. Here's Rodman, costs us a cool quarter of a million. He had a policy payable to his wife for a hundred thousand, and then another payable to some loan company to protect a loan, for a hundred and fifty thousand. And there've been a dozen like him in the last six months. How long can we keep on paying out sums like that?"

Sabin's voice replied with a trace of impatience: "What do you want me to do about it, Blakely? My God, there's an epidemic of suicide. And in a way I can't blame them. I often wonder if it's worthwhile going on like this. After you're dead, everything's peace—"

"Oh, Norman—" Wentworth recognized the voice of Mrs. Sabin, which he had heard only for a moment as they left the dining room of the Alameda Hotel—*"please* don't talk like that. You make me shiver. I—I can't sleep nights when you talk like that!"

Blake's nervous voice followed her up. "Look here, Sabin! We don't want you talking about suicide. My God, you're insured with the Orient for a quarter of a million, just like Rodman was. Look here, man, what's in your mind—?"

Sabin's high-pitched laughter cut into Blakely's question. "In my mind? Nothing at all, Blakely. Only sometimes I think there's a good reason for committing suicide. Just a single shot

Swaying with the scaffold, he fired
twice and downed both of the
thugs chasing Alma Rodman.

90

through the brain, and your troubles are over! Look at Rodman! He has nothing to worry about. It's a little bloody, I admit—"

He was interrupted by a sudden scream from Mrs. Sabin. "*Stop!* Stop, I tell you! I can't stand hearing you talk like that!"

"Perhaps," Blakely's smooth voice suggested, "your husband needs another drink. Something to pull him together."

"Yes, yes," Mrs. Sabin said eagerly. "I'll get it, Norman. The maid's off, but she left some prepared drinks in the refrigerator. I'll be right back!"

Wentworth heard her footsteps coming toward the kitchen. He stood close beside the swinging door, so that when it opened it hid him. Mrs. Sabin went directly to the refrigerator, and the door swung back.

WENTWORTH STEPPED quickly up behind her, put a hand over her mouth. He felt her jump, and pressed his hand tight against her mouth to choke off the involuntary scream that came to her lips.

"Have no fear, madam," he whispered in her ear. "I am the one you sent for!"

He released her, took a step backward.

She swayed, leaned against the refrigerator for support, and let her terror-stricken eyes wander over his person. The shock of the sudden surprise had driven every vestige of color from her cheeks. And the sinister appearance of the hatted and cloaked figure with the hideously disguised face was not very reassuring.

But Wentworth bowed to her in courtly fashion, and when he spoke his voice was soft, courteous, fear-dispelling.

"I am sorry if I frightened you, madam. It was the only way to make my presence known to you. You sent for me, and I am here. You fear that your husband may commit suicide, like Rodman and others who have done the same. Tell me quickly—What grounds have you for such a fear?"

Something in his voice, in his bearing, inspired confidence and drove away fright—in spite of his forbidding cloak and countenance.

Slowly the color returned to her face. Her lips ceased to tremble, and she managed to stand without supporting herself.

"I—I never thought the Spider would answer my appeal. I—I hardly believed you existed. But I—I was desperately afraid for my husband, so I wired." She was talking swiftly now, very low to keep the hum of their voices from being heard in the living room. "Someone is making these men commit suicide. I—I knew Selden Rodman. He loved life. He didn't want to die. Yet he killed himself. And now, my husband is talking about killing himself. Only just now—"

"I heard," Wentworth interrupted. "Have you any idea who is forcing these men to kill themselves?"

She hesitated, then said quickly: "No, no. But it's something to do with insurance. They were all insured—"

"I know that, too. Tell me—why did you meet Jack Lawson tonight?"

She started, and her eyes widened. "You—know that?"

He put out a hand, gripped her arm. "Quick! I must know if I'm to help you."

"He—he's a friend of Selden Rodman's. He phoned me when he arrived in Midwest City, and made an appointment—"

"Where did he phone you?"

"Why—right here."

"And did you go right out to meet him?"

"No. I—I remained here for most of the day—"

"You're lying, Mrs. Sabin! I arrived on the same train with Lawson. I phoned you from the station, before he did. But there was no answer. You weren't home. Why do you lie about that? Do you want me to help you?"

Suddenly she seemed to be frightened again. "Yes, yes. B-but for God's sake, don't question me! I—I can't stand your questions—"

His grip on her arm tightened. "You must answer. Why did you lie about your appointment with Lawson? He didn't phone you for an appointment. You knew he was coming to Midwest City; in fact you were expecting him. *Why did you lie about it?*"

"Leave me alone!" she wailed. "I can't tell you anymore. Leave me alone!"

Her voice had risen in pitch and suddenly the voice of Doctor Sabin called from the next room: "Elsie! For God's sake, what's the matter?"

There was the scraping of chairs, and a rush of feet toward the kitchen. Wentworth's eyes were bleak under his disguise. He had learned very little; and now his chances of learning any more were gone.

He thrust Elsie Sabin aside, pushed through the service door just as the swinging kitchen door came open to reveal the figures of Thomas Blakely and Doctor Sabin. Both had revolvers in their hands, and their eyes opened wide as they glimpsed the swishing cloak disappearing through the service door.

Blakely shouted: "The Spider! It's the Spider!" And he fired.

But Wentworth had already slammed the door, and the slug ricocheted in the kitchen. Wentworth plunged across the corridor and leaped into the service elevator, just as the kitchen door came open. Blakely and Sabin erupted into the corridor, their guns pointing toward the service elevator.

Before they could fire, Wentworth closed the door, and yanked at the lever. The cage shot downward, just as slugs from the guns of the two men shattered the door of the shaft.

WENTWORTH SWIFTLY removed his cape and hat, wiped the make-up from his face. Down in the basement he stole out into the back yard, then into the street He made his way bleak-eyed toward the Alameda Hotel. He was handicapped at every turn. Even those who might be the victims of Professor Mephisto refused to speak, or to cooperate. Whatever this hold was that Mephisto had over them, it must be broken before the Spider could make headway.

And in the meantime, he thought, Tilson's child was in the hands of Mephisto; as was also Alma Rodman—and God knew who else.

The reactions of Blakely and of Doctor Sabin upon glimpsing him were the normal reactions of respectable men. Wentworth had grown accustomed to that. Most men thought of the Spider as a dangerous man, who operated outside the law, with motives they could not understand. And what the average man cannot understand, he fears. Therefore it was natural that they should shoot at him upon finding him in the kitchen with Sabin's wife—especially when she had just raised her voice in what might be interpreted as a call for help.

That their nerves were on edge was understandable too. Sabin's conversation had indicated that he was at the breaking point; and Blakely had also sounded as if he were being driven to nervous prostration by the drain upon his company's treasury.

Although the whole matter was still beclouded in mystery, the motive of Mephisto was beginning to be cleared up a bit. There was a good deal of money involved somewhere, and it was finding its way to Professor Mephisto in some way. The blood money paid for the suicides of Rodman and those others was the prize for which Mephisto was working.

As for Elsie Sabin, Wentworth wondered why she had lied about her appointment with Jack Lawson. Perhaps he could get some information from Lawson.

He turned in at the Alameda Hotel, and inquired at the desk for the literary agent.

"He's in his room, sir," the clerk informed him. "Room Five-Six-Seven. By the way, Mr. Worth, here's a letter that was left for you by a gentlemen who did not leave his name. He said you would know about it."

Wentworth slit open the letter. It was a report, written in pencil on a sheet of paper bearing the heading: *Leffler Detective Agency,* and began:

"Report of Operative No. 14.

"Acting on instructions of our New York Correspondent, Fogarty Agency, Inc., I shadowed Paul Tilson. His actions during the day were routine, in connection with his food store business. At three-thirty p.m. he left his office and went to the Midwest Bank on Alameda Drive. I entered right behind him, and heard him say to the vice-president; 'I need a loan, Mr. Johnson. A big loan.'

"Johnson and Tilson then went into a private office and remained there a half hour. Upon leaving, I heard Johnson say to Tilson: 'Sorry, Tilson, but you can see it's impossible to give you such a big line of credit.' Tilson replied: 'Well, that leaves me only my life insurance.'

"From the bank Tilson returned to his office where he remained until five-thirty. He ate downtown, then returned to his office and worked late. He then went home. There was a crowd at his home, and he discovered that his wife had been murdered, and his little daughter kidnapped. Wife was killed by knife in back. A Chinaman of some sort was found dead beside her with a hole in his chest you could put your fist through. Mark of the Spider on Chinaman's forehead. Looks like Spider is on this case too.

"Tilson almost went nuts for a while, but he cooled off and got in his car after police were through questioning him. He drove to a parking lot on Cortlandt Avenue, and talked to some one through the fence, then he drove back to his home. The police were still there, and he did not go up, but sat in his parked car on other side of street. He is still there. I have another man working with me now, and we will stick to him. Will phone in for further instructions."

The report was signed: "Miller, Operative No. 14."

Wentworth stuffed the report in his pocket He smiled grimly. Laskar was sweating at the New York end, relaying his orders to the Leffler Agency. Laskar was doing a good job. It was a little difficult, relaying orders from Midwest City to New York, and then back to Midwest City again, but Wentworth had started at such little notice that he could not have made any better arrangements.

In a few hours, when the operatives of the Leffler Bureau began reporting direct to him, he could eliminate the necessity of relaying through Laskar. Now he had too many things to do at once. There was Jack Lawson, right here in the Alameda Hotel, who might hold the answer to a number of questions. But Paul Tilson, brooding in his car and waiting for the time when he might return to the parking lot, held greater promise. That parking lot was destroyed as far as its usefulness to Professor Mephisto was concerned. Tilson might be able to tell him all he needed to know when he learned that he would not be able to get in touch with Mephisto again.

WENTWORTH LEFT word that he would return shortly, and hurried out of the hotel. His mind was occupied with the question of who Mephisto might be in private life. That voice he had heard over the telephone in Laskar's office in New York had been the voice of an educated, cultured man. He must be someone well known in business circles, in order to be able to swing the complicated sort of deals that were indicated by the facts Wentworth had so far gleaned.

At present, the whole thing seemed to simmer down to a sort of suicide club, in which certain men were compelled to commit suicide so that Mephisto could collect their insurance. But how in the world could any man be compelled to commit suicide? Through pressure upon their families? Such had not been the case with Selden Rodman. Rodman's wife and children had been safe in a box in the Drama Theatre when the playwright killed himself.

Sabin? There appeared to be no threat of any kind to Sabin's wife.

Tilson? There was a very definite lead. In Tilson's case, the child was now being held as a hostage. Was Mephisto trying to force Tilson to commit suicide by threatening to harm or kill his child? Why, then, didn't Tilson go to the police? And how had Mephisto managed in the first place to inveigle these men into making him their beneficiary?

Wentworth suddenly snapped his fingers. The answer to the identity of Mephisto must lie in the files of the Orient Insurance Company!

Find out who had collected the insurance of those other men who were said to have committed suicide in the past few months; find out who was Selden Rodman's beneficiary—and that man would be Mephisto!

Wentworth was on Alameda Drive, walking toward Cortlandt Avenue, when this thought occurred to him. And almost at the same instant, he glimpsed Thomas Blakely, the president of the Orient Life, coming toward him. Blakely must have just left the Sabin home. He appeared greatly agitated—why not, since he had presumably just had a scuffle with the Spider! Blakely must be just as eager to solve this mystery as anyone. He would probably have the information about the beneficiaries at his fingertips.

Wentworth decided on a bold course.

He accosted Blakely. "Excuse me, sir. Aren't you Thomas Blakely, the president of the Orient Life Insurance Company?"

The stout man stared at him suspiciously, but did not recognize behind the grease paint and clever make-up the countenance of Richard Wentworth, the man to whom he had spoken in the Drama Theatre only the night before.

He said: "I don't know you, sir. But I am Blakely."

Wentworth nodded. "I was asked to look you up by a mutual friend. My name is Worth—William Worth. Mr. Richard Wentworth wired me from New York to get in touch with you."

Blakely scowled at him. "Richard Wentworth is dead."

"That's true. He wired me last night. I am anxious to find the person behind his murderer, and bring them to justice. You can help me."

Blakely did not seem eager to continue the conversation. "I'm sorry, but there isn't anything I can do for you, Mr. Worth. I know nothing of Wentworth's murder. I don't even know that he wired you—"

Wentworth leaned closer to him. "I can prove that. He told me something in his wire—something that only you and he know about."

"Well?" Impatiently.

"He told me that you mentioned to him in the Drama Theatre last night that your company was sustaining serious losses through suicides. Does that prove that I speak the truth?"

Blakely stared at Wentworth with sudden interest. "Yes," he whispered. "I did say that to him. And nobody else would know, but my wife. You interest me, Mr. Worth. Let's go where we can talk."

"No, no. I haven't the time. I want the answer to one question, and I'll be going. I'll get in touch with you later. Will you answer the question?"

"Ask it."

"Who was the beneficiary of Selden Rodman's policy with your company—and of the policies of the other men who committed suicide in the last few months?"

Blakely stared at him for a long minute. Then his mouth twitched spasmodically. He gave Wentworth a twisted smile.

"Their wives!" he said.

Wentworth's eyes narrowed. "And are their wives in town?"

"No. In each case they left on a trip. They went away to forget. You can't blame them for that. It's a horrible experience to have one's husband commit suicide."

Wentworth demanded tensely: "And have they been heard from after going away?"

"Oh, yes. Their friends receive letters regularly. There are at least three that I know of from this city, and others from various places. We know where they are all located."

"And how did you pay the claims?"

"We mailed them the papers, which they signed before notaries, and returned. Then we mailed checks in due course."

"I see," Wentworth said, disappointed. He had almost believed that he saw through the scheme. But if the widows of the suicides had not disappeared, then his theory would not hold water.

"Thanks, Mr. Blakely. May I drop in to the Orient Life and look over some of your records tomorrow?"

"With pleasure, Mr. Worth. And now, you must excuse me. I've just had a terrible experience. I was in a friend's house, when that notorious character, the Spider, paid a visit. Can you imagine it? My friend's wife screamed, and that is probably the only thing that saved her from a terrible fate. He was an awful sight to see, that Spider. But he isn't such a much. My friend and I chased him."

"Just a minute, Mr. Blakely," Wentworth urged. "One more question. Have you any idea who is back of all these suicides?"

Blakely stared at him appraisingly. Wentworth could see that there was still some reservation in the insurance company president's manner, in spite of the identification he had given of himself. The man still suspected him—of what, he could not tell. But in a situation such as this, one suspected one's best friend.

"Who is back of it?" Blakely suddenly cackled. "Who is back of it? Why, Professor Mephisto, of course! Now, Mr. Detective, you just go and find out who is Professor Mephisto—and make your will while you're doing it!"

Blakely said the last almost savagely. He swung around, hurried off down the crowded street without looking back!

CHAPTER 8
WENTWORTH SELLS HIS LIFE

WENTWORTH WATCHED him disappear in the crowd, then shrugged, and continued toward Cortlandt

Avenue. This was the queerest case he had encountered in many a day. The thing that irritated him most was that he couldn't get his teeth into it. He was convinced that he had to deal with a much cleverer antagonist than any he had heretofore encountered. Mephisto was as elusive as his crimes. Thus far, Wentworth had been compelled to fight three times for his life.

And yet, his enemy remained as nebulous as ever. His very victims refused to talk. His agents were heathens who had been brought into the country only recently, and who could probably tell very little of their master if they were examined. Perhaps they knew nothing of the real Mephisto.

They had been brought in by this person whose name appeared on the Ellis Island records as Akbar Azakan—a name which meant nothing to Wentworth, but which probably served to veil the real Mephisto from these ignorant, bloodthirsty Mongols.

And the man's diabolical cleverness was indicated by the suavity with which he had chosen a name. Mephisto! Was it the Mephistopheles of Faust that he desired to mimic? The message on the card that had been left for Tilson seemed to indicate it. Had these men sold their lives to Mephisto, just as Doctor Faustus sold his immortal soul to Mephistopheles?

It was a mad, unthinkable thing—yet it was the only supposition which the facts would support.

Wentworth approached the Tilson residence, and saw the small crowd that was still gathered around the building. A patrolman guarded the door, allowed no one to enter who did not live there.

Wentworth mingled with the crowd, and listened to the conversation. He learned that the bluecoat who had pursued the auto of the kidnappers had not been able to catch sight of them. They had made a clean escape. Then, returning, he had heard the sound of Wentworth's shot—the shot that had torn open the chest of the Mongol in the room where the dead Mrs. Tilson lay. He had been met here by a patrol car, and the officers had jointly rushed upstairs, to find Mrs. Tilson on the floor with a knife in her back, and the dead Mongol with the seal of the Spider upon his forehead.

And it seemed from the conversation he overheard that the crowd, as well as the police, was more interested in the apprehension of the Spider than in learning just what had happened. It was easier for them to assume that the Spider had killed both the woman and the Mongol. Wentworth learned that there was an alarm out for him—the Spider.

He wasn't worried about that. He had accomplished his purpose. If the police were blind, the underworld was not. Somewhere in this city, men skulked in dark corners and spoke to each other out of the sides of their mouths. From one to the other of these men the word would pass that the Spider was bucking Mephisto. And those who had reason to fear the Spider would hesitate to join Mephisto. That Mephisto would soon have to recruit new thugs, Wentworth did not doubt. He had inflicted startling losses upon the forces of the Professor, and replacements would be required. Then, when Mephisto attempted to enlist new men, he would find opposition, sullen refusal. Men would hesitate to take a job that involved bucking the Spider.

WENTWORTH WORKED his way through the crowd, down the street. He noted a small sedan at the opposite curb, and crossed over. Paul Tilson was sitting in it. He was sitting very low, with his hand over his face. But Wentworth recognized him.

Fifty feet back, another car was parked at the curb. Wentworth walked down the line, stopped alongside this second car.

There were two men in it, and they glanced at him suspiciously. Wentworth leaned in at the window, met their gaze. "Mr. Miller?" he asked.

The one at the wheel nodded. "I'm Miller. So what?"

"You left a report for me at the Alameda."

Miller brightened. "You're Mr. Worth?"

"Right. And you're Operative Fourteen, of the Leffler Detective Bureau."

"That's me!" Miller said. "We're waiting for that bloke to make a move. He's been doing nothing but mope in that car of his. By the way, I want you to meet Joe Pankin, my buddy. We're working together on this."

Wentworth nodded. "I'm going to approach Tilson. If I'm successful, I hope that we'll go somewhere together. In that event I want you two men to follow closely. *You must not lose us.* Understand? Our lives may depend upon it."

"I got you, Mr. Worth. Depend on us!"

Wentworth threw them a smile, and walked back in the direction of Tilson's car. He opened the door near the curb, and slid into the seat beside Tilson, who whirled, startled.

"W-what do you want here? Who are you?"

Wentworth met his gaze commiseratingly. "I saw your child

kidnapped, Tilson," he said softly. "I am the first person who saw your wife on the floor up there. I killed that Mongol."

Tilson's eyes widened. "T-then you're the Spider—if you're telling the truth!"

For answer, Wentworth drew from his pocket the card he had found at Mrs. Tilson's side. Tilson shuddered when he saw it, and Wentworth spoke gently.

"This card was on the floor alongside your wife's dead body. I didn't think it would be wise for the police to see it, so I took it with me. You know whom it's from?"

Tilson nodded miserably. "It's from—Professor Mephisto."

"Is that the only name you know him by?"

"That's all. That's—what he calls himself—the Devil!"

"You've had dealings with him in the past?"

"God forgive me, I have!"

"Tell me about it."

NITA VAN SLOAN

"No, no. I dare not talk. I'll have to do what he wants. It's the only way. Once you're in Mephisto's power, you're a goner!"

"Perhaps not. Perhaps I can help you. Your daughter is his prisoner. Is that the hold he has over you?"

"No, no!" Tilson groaned. "It's more than that—much more!"

"He lent you money at one time?"

Tilson jerked his head up. "How did you know that?" He studied Wentworth's features.

Wentworth shook his head. "Don't try to remember my face. It's only a borrowed face. No man has ever seen the true features of the Spider."

Tilson lowered his head, covered it with his hands. "God!" he moaned. "What will I do?"

"How much money did he lend you?" Wentworth pressed.

"Thirty thousand dollars. It was right after the crash in 1929. I would have gone to the wall. One night I was up late, trying to figure whether I could save anything from the ruin of my fortune, when the bell rang. I answered the doorbell myself, and there was a man in evening clothes, only he wore some kind of helmet with chain mail that covered his face. He had a gun and he pushed into the room. In his other hand he carried a black bag."

Tilson seemed to have suddenly lost his voice. He sat huddled in misery.

Wentworth watched him closely, his heart thumping. He knew instinctively that he was on the verge of an important disclosure.

"Go on," he urged. "Go on."

TILSON BEGAN to talk again, brokenly.

"He said his name was Mephisto, and he was there to buy my life. I thought he was crazy, but he brought out thirty thousand dollars in new one hundred dollar bills from his bag. He said they could be mine, if I'd take out a policy. I could name my own wife the beneficiary. And all I had to do was sign a note—and have my wife endorse it. He was willing to wait eight years to get his money. If I didn't make good in that time, if I couldn't pay him back, then I must commit suicide. My wife would collect the policy, and he would collect on the note from her. I was desperate, and I signed the note, got my wife to sign it too."

Tilson looked up, met Wentworth's eyes. He said tightly. *"That note was for a quarter of a million dollars!"*

Wentworth's eyes narrowed. "Mephisto was getting back *eight hundred per cent interest*—with your life in pawn to guarantee it!"

Tilson nodded. "That's right. But he made doubly sure. He made me hold a revolver in my hand for a minute. I left my fingerprints on it. The next night, a woman was found murdered in the park. She was shot with that gun. Mephisto keeps that gun in some secret place. If I don't commit suicide, he'll turn the gun over to the police. It's never too late to prosecute for murder. Can you see the web I'm in? I refused to take my life, and I couldn't raise the money to pay. I could get about a hundred thousand dollars by selling out all my interests. But that won't satisfy Mephisto. He can get a quarter of a million by forcing me to kill myself. I didn't think he'd go so far as to kidnap my child. He did more—" there was a sob in the man's voice—"he killed my wife. And I'm powerless to fight him. I've got to kill myself. I'm—going to him—to tell him I'll do it—if he'll not harm my daughter!"

Tilson was a broken man. It was easy to see that the death of his wife had been the blow that broke his spirit. Now, all his soul was wrapped up in the effort to save his daughter from death. He was licked.

Wentworth said slowly: "I think I can see a way to help you—if you'll trust me."

Tilson looked up apathetically. "I'm afraid there's no way. Mephisto is too smart—even for the Spider."

"Perhaps," Wentworth said softly. "But the Spider has done him a good deal of harm. He would be willing to sacrifice much to get his hands on the Spider. Suppose you went to him, and offered to turn the Spider over to him. Don't you think he'd trade—your life for the Spider's?"

Tilson stared at him incredulously. "You'd—do that? You'd give up your life—to save me and my daughter?"

"Well, not exactly," Wentworth told him drily. "But I'm willing to take my chance on getting out again."

Tilson seized his hand. "I—I have no right to accept this sacrifice—"

"Forget it. Go ahead now. Drive to that parking lot. I did a little shooting over there a little while ago, and the police must be still there. But I think if you drive around the block a couple of times, Mephisto's men will meet you. They won't want to lose a valuable customer like you!"

"W-what'll I tell him?"

"Tell him that you can deliver the Spider to him—in exchange for your note, your daughter, and gun with your fingerprints. He doesn't have to trust you. If he agrees to do it, you'll come back and tell me, and I'll go in with you!"

"You—you'd trust him?"

Wentworth laughed harshly. "I'll make sure he keeps his bargain!"

"All right," Tilson agreed half-heartedly. "I'll try it."

"Good. Then I'm getting out of here. I'll have you followed, of course. If Mephisto agrees to the proposition, you leave and come at once to the Alameda Hotel. Tell Mephisto you'll be back with me within a half hour. Is everything clear?"

"Y-yes."

Wentworth got out of the car. "Count fifty, then start. That will give me a chance to detail someone to follow you."

He walked swiftly back to where Miller and Pankin were waiting. "You two men follow Tilson. He's going to try to contact Mephisto, with a proposition. You've got to manage it so you won't be observed. You're not to do anything on your own initiative. When Tilson comes out of wherever he's taken, he'll drive back to the Alameda Hotel. Your job will be to make sure that nobody is following him. Understand?"

"And what do we do if he *is* followed?"

"Stop off and phone me at the Alameda. I'll be waiting in the lobby."

"Right!"

Wentworth glanced toward Tilson's car, saw that he had started, and he motioned to Miller. "Go ahead. And good luck!"

HE WATCHED the two cars disappear down the street, and then walked back swiftly toward the Alameda. At the desk he picked up two reports that had been left for him. The operative who had been tailing Jack Lawson had thought him safe in his room, but had gotten a little worried about it, and had phoned up to him, making the pretext that he was a friend from New York who had seen him in the lobby. Lawson's phone hadn't answered, and the operative had gone upstairs, picked the lock and entered. The room was vacant, and Lawson was gone. He had given the operative the slip, somehow or other!

The other report was from the operative detailed to shadow Blakely. He had lost Blakely and his wife on the way in from the airport, but had found that they were staying at their own home on the outskirts of Midwest City. This was Blakely's home town, and he had a large establishment here. The operative had ascertained that Mrs. Blakely was home, but so far Blakely himself had not returned.

Wentworth smiled. He could have told the operative that Blakely had apparently spent most of the evening with the Sabins, and had then walked down North Alameda Drive. Where he had gone after leaving Wentworth was a mystery. On a hunch, Wentworth picked up the phone and called the Leffler Bureau.

"Send one of your men to the offices of the Orient Life," he instructed. "You may find Blakely there—maybe."

"Okay, Mr. Worth!" It was Leffler himself at the phone. Apparently Fogarty in New York had impressed Leffler with the importance of this client, and he was holding down the headquarters phone himself.

"By the way, Mr. Worth," Leffler said, "I understand that the Spider is interested in this case. Now if we're bucking the Spider, I don't want any part of it—"

"Don't worry," Wentworth assured him. "You're not bucking the Spider. In fact, I want you to instruct your men that if they meet the Spider on this job, they're to cooperate with him."

"That," Leffler said softly, "is all I want to know. It's good to know just who you're working for in this game, Mr.—Worth!"

Wentworth laughed. "Don't guess too close. And let's have some action. I'm particularly anxious to get reports on where these various people are during the next hour or so. It'll help me eliminate some of them from further suspicion."

He hung up, bought a newspaper, and sat down in the lobby to read it. It was a late edition, and it carried the story of the fight at the parking lot, as well as the story of the murder of Mrs. Tilson and the kidnapping of the child. He read the paper for fifteen minutes, and then put it down. His mind was too full of this case. There were so many angles that the thing began to dance before his eyes. Mephisto's web was spread in so many directions that Wentworth could not help admiring the man's intellectual power.

Finally, he put down the paper, and went to the public telephone booths. He had been thinking of calling Laskar for an hour. He wanted to know about Nita, whether she was still safe.

He changed a five-dollar bill into silver to cover the toll call, and put through a person-to-person call. In two minutes he had Laskar on the wire.

"I haven't got much to do here, boss," Laskar told him. "I guess the Leffler people are working pretty close with you, because they haven't been phoning in here anymore."

"That's okay, Laskar. The trail is getting hotter—and dizzier. How is Miss van Sloan? Is she still at home?"

For a moment Laskar was silent. Then his voice, embarrassed, penitent, came over the wire, "Gosh, boss, I'm sorry. She came in here to the office, just when I was calling the Leffler people, in Midwest City. She knew I was talking on the long distance, and when I finished, she pulled a fast one. She said she had to call someone, and she picked up her phone. But she didn't have to call anyone. She just asked the operator how much that last call had been, and the operator asked her if she meant the Midwest City call—and there she was with the dope. She says to me: 'Laskar, is Mr. Wentworth dead, or is he in Midwest City? If he's alive and you're lying to me, I'll boil you in oil!' What could I do, boss? I—told her!"

Wentworth's knuckles whitened on the phone. "What did she do?"

"She—chartered a plane. She should have arrived in Midwest City about an hour ago. I told her your hotel, and what name you were registered under. That's what I've been worrying about. I wanted to call up and find out if she got there safely. I called the airport, and they said the plane had landed in Midwest City all right, and that she reached there. She should be at the hotel—"

"Well, she isn't!" Wentworth said coldly. "Laskar, if she's fallen into a certain person's hands, I'll do much more than boil you in oil!"

He hung up without waiting for a reply. His lips were a tight line, and his eyes were bleak. No doubt Mephisto was clever enough to have the Midwest City airport watched. If his men were watching, and recognized Nita, it could mean only one thing. And Nita hadn't reached the hotel yet. Slowly the conviction reached Wentworth that Nita van Sloan was in the hands of Mephisto.

All his planning at the penthouse apartment would be wasted. All his effort to change identities with the dead gunman would go for nothing. He paced up and down, his blood racing. It was a lucky thing for Laskar that the little ex-bookmaker was far away in New York at that moment.

CHAPTER 9
A VIEW OF INFERNO

WENTWORTH'S BITTER thoughts were interrupted by the voice of a bell boy paging Mr. Worth.

"Wanted on the phone, sir," the boy told him, when Wentworth called him over and tipped him.

Wentworth hurried to the phone, expecting a call from Miller, reporting on Tilson. But it wasn't Miller. It was New York calling, and in a moment Laskar's voice came through the receiver, quivering with excitement.

"Boss!" the bookmaker said. "Gosh, I hope you're not angry at me for telling Miss van Sloan where you went!"

"Is that what you called me for?" Wentworth asked coldly.

"No, no, boss. It's about Jack Lawson!"

"What about Jack Lawson?"

"One of Fogarty's detectives got into Lawson's room and searched it. He found letters and papers to prove that Lawson had been blackmailing Selden Rodman for years! That's why Rodman made him his literary agent. Lawson knew that Rodman had had an affair with a woman who is now married, and he was making Lawson pay at this end, and the woman at the other end. Guess who the woman is—"

"Elsie Sabin!" Wentworth snapped.

"Right, boss! How'd you guess?"

"Lawson visited her here in Midwest City, and she lied about it. Now I see why she lied."

"That's it, boss. Lawson has been having a good thing of it. According to these papers, Selden Rodman hasn't had anything to do with Elsie Sabin for years. But Lawson had a couple of pictures, and Sabin is a jealous guy. They were afraid he'd find out. Rodman was a gallant sort of guy, and he was paying Lawson to protect Mrs. Sabin, not knowing that Lawson was bleeding her at the other end!"

"Okay, Laskar. That helps a little. It explains Mrs. Sabin's reluctance to talk. Keep things humming at that end. It looks like you're getting farther than I am here."

"Gosh, boss, I wish there was something I could do to make up for telling Miss van Sloan. I'd give my right arm not to have told her—"

"That's all right, Laskar," Wentworth told him. "I don't blame you." He felt sorry now for having been so abrupt with Laskar before. The little bookmaker was loyal, and Wentworth could not find it in his heart to be angry at him. "Hang up now. I'm waiting for an important call. If all goes well, this thing will break in an hour or so."

Almost before he had racked the receiver, there was another call for him. This time it *was* Miller.

"All set, Mr. Worth!" Miller told him excitedly. "Pankin and

I followed Tilson. Two guys in a Ford car picked him up, and he left his own car and got in the Ford. They drove him around to the back of that old brewery, and went in through the basement. He stayed there for about twenty minutes. He just came out, and he's on the way back to the hotel."

Wentworth's eyes were glistening. If Mephisto had accepted the offer Tilson had made, things would come to a head. "Fine!" he exclaimed. "Come to the Alameda as quickly as possible!"

He left the phone, went upstairs to his room. Here he worked swiftly. From an inner pocket he took his flat black case of tools. Resting under a strap in this container was an object that resembled a small cigar. Wentworth examined it, handling it gingerly, and then placed it in his breast pocket. He left his kit of tools in the room, and descended into the lobby. At the cigar counter, he bought three cigars about the same size as the object he had taken from his tool kit, and placed them in his pocket alongside it. Now it seemed to all intents that he had four cigars in his breast pocket.

He had hardly finished, when Paul Tilson came striding into the lobby, looking flushed and excited. Behind him came Miller and Pankin.

Tilson saw Wentworth, and came up to him, breathing hard. "It's all arranged! Mephisto promises to give me back the incriminating gun with my fingerprints, to release my daughter, and to return the note I signed—if I will bring the Spider. But you must allow yourself to be searched before entering their place, and if you are carrying guns they will be taken from you.

Outside of that Mephisto says he will exact no promise from you. He says it won't be necessary."

There was a chill at Wentworth's heart as he heard that last. He had a good idea why Mephisto thought it unnecessary to exact any further promises. If he had Nita, he must have guessed that Richard Wentworth had not died at the penthouse fight in New York. And he must indeed be sure of himself.

WENTWORTH PUSHED those thoughts from his mind. He swung to Miller and Pankin. "I want two guns. Can you spare them?"

Both operatives had extra guns, and each gave him one. Wentworth ejected the cartridges from both guns, then took his own fully loaded automatics from his shoulder holsters, and gave them to Tilson.

"Keep them in your pocket," he instructed. "They've already searched you, haven't they?"

Tilson shook his head. "They never bother to search me. They aren't afraid of me at all."

Wentworth nodded. He placed the two empty guns in his holsters, made sure that the four cigars were in place in his breast pocket, and started for the door.

"Follow us," he instructed Miller, "but don't keep too close, and don't interfere, no matter what happens. Cruise around outside the brewery, and be ready for a getaway."

Miller protested. "Why don't you call in the cops? As long as we know where this Mephisto's hangout is, why don't we raid it?"

"No, no!" Tilson almost shouted. "My God, I'm not the only one involved in this. Mephisto has other hostages there. Dozens of men would be ruined, and Mephisto would destroy that whole crowd if there was a raid. All those women and children would be dead before the police could get in. You've got to promise not to call the police!"

"We won't," Wentworth assured him. "We're going to try to handle this as a personal matter—and God help us if there's a slip!"

He went out with Tilson, but did not let him take his car. Instead, he found John Grant, the cab driver he had used earlier in the evening. Grant had been parked in front of the hotel all this time, as per instructions. His faith in Wentworth was demonstrated by the fact that his clocks read $4.30 for waiting time.

Wentworth instructed him to drive to within a block of the rear entrance of the brewery. "Here's another twenty-dollar bill. When we get out, I want you to drive away without looking back at us. Think you can do that?"

"Sure. I'll keep my eyes straight front!"

Wentworth had had a purpose in making that peculiar request. Tilson watched him with wondering eyes, as he set about using his make-up kit. In a few moments he was transformed from William Worth into—the Spider!

Once more he produced the cloak and hat, and donned them. Tilson breathed a thin sigh. "I'd never have thought it possible! You've changed completely. I—I almost feel as if I was sitting next to a different man!"

Wentworth said nothing. He was going over in his mind all

the possibilities of a slip. There might be many, but he had to chance them.

At last the cab stopped, and Wentworth and Tilson got out. True to his promise, Grant drove away without looking behind. They were on North Van Wyck Avenue now, a block from North Cortlandt. Down the street they could see the boarded-up rear wall of the brewery. Behind them they could see the bulk of Miller's car, crawling at a snail's pace.

"Let's go!" Wentworth commanded. "And remember—when I say—'Guns!'—you hand me both those automatics—and do it fast!"

As they walked slowly toward the brewery, Tilson said: "There is an underground passage leading from the parking lot on North Cortlandt, into the building. But with the police in charge over there, they've been compelled to use this direct entrance."

Wentworth nodded. "That passage is reached through the shed in the rear, isn't it?"

"Yes. How do you know all these things—?"

"That's how Alma Rodman must have disappeared. They must have seized her when she reached the shed."

As they approached the brewery, a cellar door, which had been flush with the street, was lifted open, and the head of a Mongol appeared. He motioned for them to descend.

THIS WAS a ticklish moment, one which Wentworth feared. Would Mephisto order him killed out of hand, or would he have him brought into his presence? Wentworth banked on the vanity which he knew all criminals to possess. Mephisto knew that the Spider was giving himself up to save a child. He would want to gloat over the Spider. But there was an element of doubt. Mephisto had proved himself different from the average breed of criminal in everything else. Would he be different in this, too?

Wentworth led the way, and Tilson followed. There was a squeaking wooden staircase down into the cellar, and at the foot of it four Mongols were waiting. At once the cellar door was shut over their heads, leaving the cellar in pitch darkness; but only for a moment.

Immediately, electric lights sprang into life. Wentworth looked around and saw that they were in a small room, but that an open door led into another portion of the cellar. It was surprisingly hot here.

Tilson must also have noticed the heat, for he said with an effort at lightness: "Just like hell, isn't it?"

Wentworth didn't answer. He was staring at the four Mongols. Three of them were no different than those he had encountered in New York. They were dressed in ordinary Western clothes, and each had a knife in a sheath attached to his belt.

It was the fourth Mongol who held his gaze. This man was clad in baggy pantaloons, a scarlet jacket opened down the front, revealing the hideous figures that had been painted on his chest. His headdress was a medieval helmet decorated with shrunken human ears. This man was gazing at Wentworth with bloodshot, hot eyes that mirrored a burning hate.

Wentworth was taut. This man, he guessed, was the Akbar Azakan who had furnished bond for the others. He was dressed in a manner to suggest that he was a priest, or *shaman* of the Buriat tribes. But Wentworth had lived and worked in the section around Lake Baikal for almost two years before the United States entered the World War. He had been assigned to the British Intelligence, lent to them by the United States Intelligence, as one of the few white men who could speak the Buriat dialects. He was intimately familiar with the tenets of *Shamanism,* had seen their services and their priests. He recognized this one at once for a fraud. That these other Buriat Mongols allowed themselves to be deceived by him was not strange. They were willing to believe anything as long as they were fed and clothed, and paid.

Wentworth smiled at the Mongol Shaman. But his smile hid the tautness of his muscles. Would they fall upon them now with their knives?

All four of them were fingering the carved handles of their daggers. And these Buriats were no mean opponents when armed with knives, as he had reason to know from his experience in New York.

The Mongol Shaman stared at him with concentrated hate. "You are the Spider!" he said at last. "You are the one who killed my men!"

Wentworth nodded. He saw that the bogus priest was talking for effect, for the purpose of stirring up the other three Mongols. Perhaps he wanted the Spider killed quickly for his own reasons.

Wentworth spoke in the Buriat dialect "You are the one who is known as Akbar Azakan. But you are no *shaman.* The priests of the Buriats are holy men, and not charlatans and murderers. You will bring disgrace and shame upon the Buriat nation!"

The Mongol Shaman snarled. "Quiet! Were it not for the

commands of Mephisto, we would dispatch you at once. Raise your hands, that we may search you for weapons!"

Wentworth complied, and one of the Mongols stepped forward, went thoroughly through his clothes. He saw the cigars, but did not disturb them. He found the two empty guns in Wentworth's holsters, and triumphantly removed them.

None of them bothered to search Tilson. They seemed to consider him a harmless nonentity.

During the search of Wentworth, the Mongols had so maneuvered as to crowd Tilson into a far corner, away from the Spider. Wentworth's eyes were narrowed, watching the *shaman*. The Mongols whose greasy hands had just finished pawing his clothes seemed to be taut, awaiting a signal of some sort.

And that signal came.

Akbar's voice came in a screech, in the Buriat dialect.

"Kill him, my men! Drive your knives into his body!"

Wentworth had been expecting just such an order from the *shaman;* in fact, he had read the intent of the Mongols even while they searched him. As the knives flashed toward him, he swished his black cloak about him, and spun around in a swift pirouette. The lunging knives, caught in the folds of the cloak, were deflected. One blade gashed Wentworth's left arm, another ripped through the cloak. The third Mongol had lunged at Wentworth's throat, but the blade slithered past harmlessly.

Wentworth dropped to his knees, wrapped his arms around the legs of the Mongol in front of him, and yanked hard. The man fell forward, and Wentworth heaved up to his feet again, raising the other into the air, kicking and clawing. The other two dived in once more with their knives, and Wentworth literally hurled his Mongol at them, sending them all flailing backward in a struggling heap on the floor.

Akbar Azakan stood near the door, screeching imprecations at his men, shouting to them to return to the attack. He raised a knife.

Wentworth dived across the floor, past the squirming group of Mongols, directly at the *shaman,* in a swift, running tackle, and the *shaman's* knife slithered through the air above his head.

His shoulder caught the *shaman* in the legs, sent him crashing backward through the open doorway, into the next room. Behind him he suddenly heard Tilson shout frenziedly: *"Look out, Spider!"*

He catapulted to his feet, swung around in time to meet a second concerted rush. They were coming at him now, their knives held low. Their eyes were gleaming hotly, and he could see the glistening beads of perspiration on their faces and throats.

Tilson was separated from him by the entire width of the room. There would be no chance for the bewildered man to get his automatics to him. He must meet the knives of these Mongols with nothing but his wits and his agility.

He had time for that single glance, and then the Buriats were upon him, coming in from three directions. He leaped backward, felt the wall behind him, braced himself against it, and brought up his right foot in the swift, deadly blow of the *savate.* The tip of his shoe caught the Mongol's wrist, and there was a sharp, unmistakable snapping of bone. The man screamed.

Wentworth hurled himself directly at the second, coming

in from the left. He caught the man's knife hand in a vise-like, overhand grip, and brought up his right fist in a powerful, smashing blow to the point of the man's jaw. The Mongol's head snapped back sickeningly, and he collapsed.

Wentworth sensed the presence of the third Mongol behind him, and his quick sidestep action saved his life, for the Mongol had been about to plunge a knife between his shoulder blades. The blade swished harmlessly through the air, and before the man had recovered his balance, Wentworth was on his feet once more, gripping a knife picked up from the floor.

The Mongol recovered his balance, saw that Wentworth was armed, and switched his grip from the handle to the blade, raised it to throw.

But Wentworth had caught a glimpse of the *shaman,* coming back into the room through the open doorway, and he leaped straight at Akbar. The *shaman* attempted to flee, but Wentworth caught him by the arm, drew him close, and pressed the point of his knife against the bogus high priest's throat.

He said in the Buriat dialect "Call off your war-dog, Akbar!"

The *shaman* shrank from the point of Wentworth's blade, which was pricking his throat. He called out hoarsely: "Stop, Atakai! Drop thy knife!"

The man, Atakai, slowly lowered his arm, let the knife slip to the floor.

Wentworth grunted his satisfaction. "Good! I could kill you, Akbar, but I came to see Mephisto. Take me to him!"

Akbar Azakan bowed his submission, though his wicked eyes glittered with hate. "I yield. Follow me."

"I will!" Wentworth told him. "With this knife at your spine!"

He made the man, Atakai, lead the way, with Tilson bringing up the rear. They passed through two corridors, and brought up short at a turn in the hallway.

Akbar Azakan turned slowly, and said: "We come to the presence of Mephisto. But you may not appear before him armed. Give me the knife. I do not go in with you. Atakai will accompany you, and he is unarmed also. I give you my word that I will not attack you again." His lips curled. "I leave you to the much tenderer mercies of Mephisto. Perhaps you will wish that you had died back there—before Mephisto is finished with you!"

Wentworth grinned. "Walk back to the end of the corridor. I'll throw the knife to you. I promised to visit Mephisto without weapons, and I'll keep that promise!"

Akbar's eyes were gleaming cunningly. He bowed low, backed away down to the end of the corridor. Wentworth slid the knife along the floor to him. Akbar picked it up, threw him a queer look, then turned and disappeared down the corridor, without a word. Wentworth glanced at Tilson, who was shivering as with the ague, then looked at Atakai.

"All right," he said simply. "I'm ready to talk to your august master!"

The Mongol glowered at him, then turned and led the way around the bend in the corridor. They passed through an unoccupied room, then stopped at the threshold of an amazing chamber, the like of which Wentworth had never seen before in his life.

There had apparently been a good deal of work done in the

cellar of this old brewery. This room must have been the boiler room at one time. Half the floor was raised about ten feet above the other half. The lower portion must have housed the boiler.

Upon the raised portion stood the figure of Mephisto.

Wentworth stopped in the doorway and gazed at his antagonist. Mephisto still wore his faultless evening clothes, and the helmet with the chain-mail. Nothing of his face showed except his eyes; and those eyes met Wentworth's in a steady, appraising glance.

Both men stood still and studied each other. At last Mephisto spoke. "That is a good disguise, Richard Wentworth. I don't wonder that people fear you. You have made your face ugly, and that cloak and hat are enough to cause fear alone. But without your automatics, I am afraid that you are harmless."

Wentworth bowed, never taking his eyes from the other. "That is to be seen, Mephisto. Since we are exchanging compliments, let me say that you are far above the average criminal whom I have encountered. You have a mentality capable of greater things than crime."

Mephisto's voice was an open sneer. "I am doing well enough, thank you. Won't you step in?"

Wentworth obeyed, and saw now what had been hidden from him while he was at the doorway; he got a glimpse down into the pit that formed the other half of the room.

More than a dozen women and children crouched down there, in utter, agonized silence. They stared up in hopeless resignation.

They sat on the hard stone floor, but that floor wasn't cold.

For in the center of the pit, there was a depression some five feet square, which formed a sort of secondary pit. And in that secondary pit Wentworth could see a seething mass of molten metal of some sort. It was white hot, and almost seemed to be alive. Two of the Mongols were stirring the metal. The heat emanating from that metal fairly scorched the women and children down there.

Wentworth recognized Tilson's daughter among the captives, as well as Alma Rodman. His own cheeks were hot from the heat down there, and he could imagine how scorched those poor women and children must be.

Mephisto must have read his thoughts, for he laughed. "You see, Spider, I have created a sort of private hell for these people. They are paying for the sins of others!"

"For the sins of the poor fools whom you tempted, Professor Mephisto!" Wentworth said bitterly. "I know how you bought the lives of their husbands and fathers, and framed them so that they could never get free of you. You forced their men to commit suicide, and then you brought the wives here. You probably had them write letters to their relatives, which you mailed from various parts of the country. In that way you kept the police from being brought into the case to search for missing persons."

Mephisto bowed. "You have thought it out very accurately, Mr. Spider. Perhaps you know more?"

"I do. I know that you are making eight hundred percent interest on your investment, taking the lives of men as your security. You forced Selden Rodman to commit suicide in order to save himself from being framed for murder, and to save his wife from this hell. But you've put her here anyway, I see."

"True, Mr. Spider. She must turn over the proceeds of the Rodman policy to me. It is too bad, Mr. Spider, that you had to interfere. I am sorry that you must die. But I cannot allow you to stop me from becoming the richest man in America. You see, when I have done collecting on my loans, I will have some hundred million dollars!"

"The Devil's Pawnbroker, eh!" Wentworth taunted. He was deliberately goading the other on to talk. Mephisto was consciously disguising his voice behind that mask of chain mail, and Wentworth felt that if he could make him talk a little longer, he would recognize the voice.

But Mephisto was no fool. "Enough of this!" he exclaimed. "Are you ready to die, Spider?"

"If you are ready to release Tilson and his daughter."

"On the contrary, I will do no such thing. Now that I have you safe, my Spider, Tilson will pay in full—either in cash, or with his life, or with the life of his daughter!"

Paul Tilson grew pale. "But you promised, Mephisto! You promised to free my daughter—"

"You were a fool to believe me, Tilson," Mephisto said softly. "And so was the Spider!"

He motioned to the single Mongol who stood guard at the door, and the Buriat drew his knife, stepped close to Wentworth. "Spider, you are about to die—"

CHAPTER 10
THE FACE OF MEPHISTO

W ENTWORTH WAS standing tautly alongside of Tilson. Out of the corner of his eyes he saw the Buriat raise his knife.

He shouted: "The guns, Tilson!" and at the same time he whipped his hat, flicked it into the Mongol's eyes. The man yelled more with the surprise of the thing than with pain. For the moment he was blinded, and Wentworth dropped the hat, seized his knife hand, twisted with merciless viciousness. The man screamed as his arm went up behind his back in a swift, punishing hammerlock.

Wentworth pushed hard, and the knife flew out of his hand. The Mongol went hurtling into air, over the side of the platform, and Wentworth snatched the two guns that Tilson was extending to him. With a flick of the wrist he had Mephisto covered.

Down in the pit below the Mongol had gone hurtling directly into the vat of molten metal, and he uttered a single terrible scream, then gurgled and was silent. There was a hissing sound, and the revolting stench of burned flesh.

Wentworth covered Mephisto. "Put your hands up, or I'll kill you!" he ordered.

The women and children in the pit below were screaming their horror at the sudden, terrible death of the Mongol. The place was a bedlam of noise. But Mephisto did not move to raise his hands in obedience to Wentworth's order. In fact he was laughing through his chain mail.

And Wentworth realized that Mephisto still held all the advantage. Tilson had realized it too, for he frantically gripped Wentworth's arm even as Wentworth sent the Mongol spinning off the platform.

"For God's sake, don't shoot him!" Tilson shouted. "Fifty men will be disgraced if he dies. He still has the evidence against them locked away somewhere!"

Wentworth grimly pushed him off. "He'll turn the evidence over. Mephisto, you know the Spider's word is good. I give you my word that I'll shoot you in cold blood if you don't—"

"Wait!" Mephisto's voice rang out in loud desperation. "Don't say it, Spider, till you have seen what I have to show you!"

Wentworth paused, and he suddenly felt a cold chill. He had a premonition of what was coming.

Mephisto, utterly regardless of the Mongol who had just died horribly, stepped to the wall at his right, where there was a small aperture. "Look!" he said dramatically.

Wentworth kept him covered, stepped close to the aperture, and glanced swiftly through it. His blood raced, pounded through his head. The thing he feared had come. Mephisto had planned with diabolical cleverness. He had allowed for Wentworth's gaining the upper hand, and he had kept himself an ace in the hole.

That aperture afforded a view of another room. A giant treadmill had been set up in there, and beneath it there was another vat of the molten metal, similar to the one in the pit. The treadmill was moving slowly around, and chained to a bolt through its center was Nita van Sloan!

Suddenly, glancing up, Wentworth saw Mephisto leveling his machine gun.

She was so placed upon the treads of the wheel that when it rolled down she would be dropped into the vat of metal that hissed directly below her. By continually climbing up the treads, she could prevent herself from falling. But if it kept up for long, she would become exhausted, and would fall.

The horror of it struck at Wentworth like a blow. He clamped his lips tight, turned away from the aperture.

Mephisto's voice mocked him. "Stalemate, eh, Spider? What price are you willing to pay for Miss van Sloan's release from her precarious position?"

"What do you want?" Wentworth asked dully.

"You will give up your guns, which you so cleverly planted with Tilson. That is all I ask. I will then amuse myself by setting my Mongols upon you with their knives. It will be interesting to see how long you can defend yourself against them—with your bare hands. When you give up your guns, Miss van Sloan will be freed from the treadmill."

Wentworth shook his head. "No. Release her first. Give her paper and pencil. When she is free—in the street—she will send back a note with one of your Buriats that she is absolutely safe; and I'll give up my guns. The Spider promises!"

Mephisto did not hesitate. "Your word is good, Spider!"

HE STEPPED to the aperture, while Wentworth still kept him covered, and he called down to someone in the other room. He waited a moment, then sighed with regret. "It is too bad that I could not continue the experiment with Miss van Sloan." He shrugged. "Well, I'll try it with one of the others some time."

He stepped back from the aperture again, waved a hand nonchalantly. "She is free, Spider!"

Wentworth threw a swift glance into the other room, saw that Nita was freed of her bonds, standing clear of the treadmill, and looking up toward him.

He called out to her: "Nita, dear, they'll give you paper and pencil, and they'll take you out. Go to the Alameda Hotel. When you're safe there, write a note and give it to them to bring back to me. Now go."

Nita must have guessed the sacrifice he was making for her. She stamped her foot. "I won't go, Dick! You ran out on me once. If you're going to die again, I'll die with you!"

She was weak from her exertion on the treadmill, but there was spirit and determination in her voice.

Mephisto shrugged. "Stalemate again, Spider? What will you do now?"

"This," said Wentworth. He reached with his left hand through the aperture, called out: "Nita! Catch!" and threw one of his automatics in a wide arc, aiming accurately so that it would come within reach.

The gun arced through the air, and Nita reached out, caught it, before those in the room with her realized what was happening. The Mongols in the next room rushed at her with knives, but she faced them, gun in hand. They crowded back.

"Good boy, Dick!" she called up to him. "Now we can both go out fighting!"

"Hold them if you can, Nita!" he shouted to her. He swung

on Mephisto. "Order those two Mongols down there to allow the women and children to come up out of the pit!"

Mephisto said bitingly: "How do you expect to get them out of here? And what about the incriminating evidence that I have locked up—the evidence that will bring disgrace—"

"Never mind!" Wentworth rapped. "I'll attend to that when the time comes. Do as I say!"

Mephisto shrugged. "As you will!"

He addressed the two Mongols in the pit, and they bowed, moved to one side, and motioned the women and children toward the ladder leading up to the platform.

The poor captives uttered shouts of joy, and began to climb the ladder. Wentworth kept Mephisto covered until the last one was up. Then he called to them: "Get out of here. See if you can reach the next room. I'll—"

He had neglected to take account of one element—the cowardly desperation of Paul Tilson. Tilson had been standing silent at his side all this time. Now he shouted: "No, no! You'll ruin me, and everyone else! We've got to do what Mephisto says!"

And Tilson threw both arms around Wentworth's gun hand, hugged it hard to his chest. Wentworth's arm was twisted downward. He heaved against Tilson, but the man clung with mad desperation. And as he held on, the Mongol Shaman with half a dozen of his Buriats streamed into the room. They swarmed over Wentworth, and one of them struck his wrist with the hilt of a knife. The gun was knocked out of Wentworth's hand.

Mephisto was shouting: "Take him alive! I want him for the metal vat!"

Tilson let go his grip, and the Buriats formed a vicious circle around Wentworth, their knives gleaming. At one spot the circle was incomplete, and in the opening stood Mephisto, holding a submachine gun in the crook of his arm. One of the Mongols had guns, and Mephisto shouted to him: "If you must shoot him, hit him in the leg. Don't kill him—yet!"

Wentworth stood stock still in the center of that grim circle. He was crouching as if about to do battle. In reality he knew the hopelessness of such an idea, but there was a definite purpose in his attitude. The Mongols had forgotten the pitiful group of women and children on the platform, and they were concentrating all their attention upon him.

And the captives were taking advantage of this lack of attention on the part of the Mongols. They were streaming swiftly out of the room, into the passage outside. Wentworth hoped that they would be able to find a means of escape.

HE STOOD that way, holding the attention of the Mongols, for perhaps two minutes; and then, when the last of the captives had streamed from the room, he relaxed, and the bitter, soul-chilling laughter of the Spider filled the room.

The Mongols looked at one another, and shrugged. The Mongol *Shaman* stepped close to Mephisto. "He laughs, Professor. The Spider laughs. Let us make him beg for mercy!"

Before Mephisto could reply, Wentworth spoke. He used the Buriat dialect, so that the Mongols could understand. He had taken the cigar-shaped object from his pocket.

"Shall I tell you why the Spider laughs? For the Spider has taken an oath never to be the prisoner of an enemy. The Spider has sworn to die when that time comes. And now the Spider shall die!"

He paused, fingering the cigar-shaped object. *"But you shall all die with the Spider!"*

Suddenly there was silence. Mephisto shifted uncomfortably, watching Wentworth's hands.

Wentworth went on. "This object which I hold is not what it appears to be. It is a platinum vial. It is divided into two compartments by a thin filament of wax. In one of the compartments is a chemical known as—" he switched to the English word—*"nitrogen iodide.* In the other compartment, separated only by the filament of wax, is *free oxygen.* Should this vial fall from my hand, as I hold it now, the wax filament would break, thus permitting the *nitrogen iodide* to mingle with the *free oxygen.* "

He paused, watching the puzzlement in the faces of the Mongols. "Professor Mephisto will tell you what will happen when the two chemicals mingle!"

The Mongols all turned to look at Mephisto. For once the man in the mask of mail had nothing to say. He stood silent, cuddling his submachine gun.

"Now my friends," Wentworth continued, still employing the Buriat dialect, "if you all wish to be torn to pieces by one of the most powerful explosives known to man, all you need to do is try to stop me!"

Slowly, facing the Mongols he began to move toward the door, holding the vial between the thumb and forefinger of his left hand. The Mongols, with distended eyes, moved gingerly aside to let him pass.

Mephisto called out: "Spider! Wait! Do you give me your word that that vial contains the things you mentioned?"

The Spider smiled sardonically. "I invite you to find out for yourself, Professor Mephisto!" He stooped, picked up his gun, then backed out of the room. No one attempted to stop him. He saw Tilson, standing open-mouthed in the room, and ordered him: "Come on, Tilson, if you want to come. Of course, if you'd rather stay—"

Tilson yelped, and darted after him. Swiftly they hurried down the corridor toward the room where they had seen Nita. They reached it just in time to see Nita leveling her gun at a group of Mongols facing her, while the captive women and children watched, spellbound. The Mongols started to rush Nita, and Wentworth yelled to her: "This way! Quick!"

Nita heard him, fired a single shot at the Mongols, then turned and ran toward him swiftly. At the same time Wentworth heard Akbar Azakan exhorting the Mongols in the other room to attack Wentworth.

"Have no fear, children!" the Mongol *Shaman* was saying. "I will invoke the good spirits, and the Spider will be helpless to harm you. Attack! Kill!"

He was brave, now that he was no longer in personal danger. His men would go against Wentworth and they could get their heads blown off for all he cared.

Wentworth faced the corridor from which he had just come

in time to see the first of the Mongols appear, armed with guns and knives.

His eyes grew cold and bleak, and his lips thinned to a tight line. "I hate to do this, Nita," he said. "But it's they or us!"

He threw the nitrogen iodide vial.

IT STRUCK the wall, at the other end of the room. There was a terrific detonation that shook the building, and flames burst out, enveloping the first of the Mongols. They pushed back, screaming, while the Mongols who were already in this room uttered screams of rage, and rushed at Wentworth.

He snatched his second gun from Nita's hand, shouted to her: "Get the women and kids out of here!"

Nita needed no second order. She began herding the captives out, while Wentworth, his cloak flapping wide, stood spraddle-legged, his two guns blazing at the oncoming Mongols, while flames blazed from the living inferno where he had flung the bomb.

And now, from another doorway, Akbar Azakan appeared, leading a group of Mongols. They were shouting, screaming, in a paroxysm of fanaticism. Akbar held a knife in his fingers, by the hilt, and he raised it to hurl as he ran. Wentworth shot him through the head, and the bogus priest fairly bounced into the air, then fell to the floor.

Up at the left, there was a small balcony, which might once have been an engineer's platform. Suddenly, glancing up, Wentworth saw Mephisto appear there, with his submachine gun.

The professor shouted to the Mongols to head off the escaping women and children, while he himself beaded the gun upon

Wentworth. His first spray was wild, and he never got a chance to send a second. Wentworth snapped up one of his guns, placed a slug through his throat, just where it showed beneath his chain mail.

Mephisto dropped the machine gun, sagged across the rail of the balcony, and then slid slowly over, to fall to the floor with a resounding thump.

Now, the shrieks of police whistles and the blasting of radio car sirens filled the air. Wentworth held his ground in the building, which had become a roaring furnace now. His automatics were empty, and he was desperately reloading for the next rush of the Mongols. But all the fight was taken out of the Buriats. Their priest and their Mephisto was dead. The police were coming. Suddenly they turned tail and ran toward the side door, away from the flames, and away from the awesome figure of the Spider.

In a moment the cellar was clear.

Wentworth turned, saw that all the captives were safely out. The flames were spreading, would soon reach the helmeted body of Mephisto. Suddenly, Nita van Sloan appeared in the doorway. She had gotten all the captives out, and she was back to see how Wentworth was faring.

She came to him, and he took her in his arms. "Nita!" he exclaimed. "This was about the closest!"

She looked up at him, and she was beautiful, with cheeks flushed by the crackling flames.

"The police are coming, Dick."

He nodded. "That means the Spider must go. This building is doomed. Whatever evidence Mephisto had here will be destroyed."

A whistle shrilled outside.

"Don't—don't you want," she stammered, "to see who he is—that Mephisto?"

Slowly they crossed the floor toward the searing flames. Wentworth stooped beside the dead body of Professor Mephisto, and removed the helmet. For the first time they saw Mephisto without his mask.

Nita did not recognize him. "Who is it, Dick?"

His voice was somber. "It's Doctor Norman Sabin. It was he who advanced money to all those men. He used his inside knowledge of the insurance business to insure them. He made Rodman commit suicide because the playwright had had an affair with his wife. They didn't know he knew, but he did. And he was vengeful."

"But—Dick! It was Mrs. Sabin who sent you that telegram!"

Wentworth laughed bitterly. "Mephisto overreached himself that time. To divert suspicion from himself, he pretended that he too was contemplating suicide. His wife got scared and sent for me!"

She raised her eyes to his. "Oh, Dick! Why must there be such people in the world?"

He shrugged. "There are, and it can't be helped. And that's why—" he stooped and swiftly planted the livid seal upon Mephisto's forehead—"that's why the Spider can't quit!"

He stood up, took Nita's hand, and the two of them hurried out through the side exit of the building, faded into the night.

Behind them, the funeral pyre of Professor Mephisto blazed into the sky....

POPULAR HERO PULPS AVAILABLE NOW:

THE SECRET 6
- ❏ #1: The Red Shadow — $13.95
- ❏ #2: House of Walking Corpses — $13.95
- ❏ #3: The Monster Murders — $13.95
- ❏ #4: The Golden Alligator — $13.95

OPERATOR 5
- ❏ #1: The Masked Invasion — $13.95
- ❏ #2: The Invisible Empire — $13.95
- ❏ #3: The Yellow Scourge — $13.95
- ❏ #4: The Melting Death — $13.95
- ❏ #5: Cavern of the Damned — $13.95
- ❏ #6: Master of Broken Men — $13.95
- ❏ #7: Invasion of the Dark Legions — $13.95
- ❏ #8: The Green Death Mists — $13.95
- ❏ #9: Legions of Starvation — $13.95
- ❏ #10: The Red Invader — $13.95
- ❏ #11: The League of War-Monsters — $13.95
- ❏ #12: The Army of the Dead — $13.95
- ❏ #13: March of the Flame Marauders — $13.95
- ❏ #14: Blood Reign of the Dictator — $13.95
- ❏ #15: Invasion of the Yellow Warlords — $13.95
- ❏ #16: Legions of the Death Master — $13.95
- ❏ #17: Hosts of the Flaming Death — $13.95
- ❏ #18: Invasion of the Crimson Death Cult — $13.95
- ❏ #19: Attack of the Blizzard Men — $13.95
- ❏ #20: Scourge of the Invisible Death — $13.95
- ❏ #21: Raiders of the Red Death — $13.95
- ❏ #22: War-Dogs of the Green Destroyer — $13.95
- ❏ #23: Rockets From Hell — $13.95
- ❏ *NEW:* #24: War-Masters from the Orient — $13.95

DUSTY AYRES AND HIS BATTLE BIRDS
- ❏ #1: Black Lightning! — $13.95
- ❏ #2: Crimson Doom — $13.95
- ❏ #3: The Purple Tornado — $13.95
- ❏ #4: The Screaming Eye — $13.95
- ❏ #5: The Green Thunderbolt — $13.95
- ❏ #6: The Red Destroyer — $13.95
- ❏ #7: The White Death — $13.95
- ❏ #8: The Black Avenger — $13.95
- ❏ #9: The Silver Typhoon — $13.95
- ❏ #10: The Troposphere F-S — $13.95
- ❏ #11: The Blue Cyclone — $13.95
- ❏ #12: The Tesla Raiders — $13.95

MAVERICKS
- ❏ #1: Five Against the Law — $12.95
- ❏ #2: Mesquite Manhunters — $12.95
- ❏ #3: Bait for the Lobo Pack — $12.95
- ❏ #4: Doc Grimson's Outlaw Posse — $12.95
- ❏ #5: Charlie Parr's Gunsmoke Cure — $12.95

THE MYSTERIOUS WU FANG
- ❏ #1: The Case of the Six Coffins — $12.95
- ❏ #2: The Case of the Scarlet Feather — $12.95
- ❏ #3: The Case of the Yellow Mask — $12.95
- ❏ #4: The Case of the Suicide Tomb — $12.95
- ❏ #5: The Case of the Green Death — $12.95
- ❏ #6: The Case of the Black Lotus — $12.95
- ❏ #7: The Case of the Hidden Scourge — $12.95

Printed in Great Britain
by Amazon

47540464R00090